A JUDY BOLTON MYSTERY

THE MIDNIGHT VISITOR

BY

MARGARET SUTTON

AUTHOR OF
THE HAUNTED ATTIC
THE MAGIC MAKERS, ETC.

ILLUSTRATED BY

PELAGIE DOANE

GROSSET & DUNLAP
PUBLISHERS   NEW YORK

To Ramona Kessinger,
A Frequent and Most Welcome Visitor

CONTENTS

ALMOST ANYTHING COULD BE HIDDEN UNDER THOSE
GHOSTLY COVERS.

The Midnight Visitor

THE
MIDNIGHT VISITOR

CHAPTER I

THE patter of rain on the window and the tapping of the typewriter keys made a curious rhythm as Judy Bolton typed away at her desk in one corner of Peter Dobbs' little law office in Roulsville.

"I think I'd hate anything but a noisy machine," she said. "There's something so comforting about the tapping of the keys."

Peter merely grinned at her, keeping his thoughts to himself. He was such an odd combination—half the serious lawyer that he tried to be and the other half simply a grown-up little boy. Judy could still imagine him sharing his huge slices of bread and jam with her in his grandmother's kitchen. It was nice being his secretary now and working in the town where

1

they had played together as children. She finished the last of the letters he had dictated and then walked over to his desk.

"What next?" she asked. "Is there any more correspondence or shall I go ahead with those pamphlets on wills?"

"You might as well go ahead with the pamphlets," he began, but the jangling of the telephone at his elbow interrupted him.

Judy paid very little attention to the conversation. She had been anxious to get back to the pamphlets. They fascinated her. Wills were such mysterious things. She could hear Peter now, over the telephone, promising to give somebody one of the pamphlets on wills that she was preparing. She had made several copies on the typewriter, punched holes in them and tied them with blue silk cord. They did look nice. She stacked them in a neat pile and, as soon as he had finished telephoning, took them over to him to show them off. The rain outside beat against the window so loudly that she could hardly hear him talk.

"That's just fine!" he shouted above the noise of the storm. "Keep out one of them for Harry Vincent and then, if he isn't here within half an hour, we'll close up the office and drive home."

"Harry Vincent!" Judy exclaimed, remembering him only too well from past experiences. "I thought he had left this part of the country for good."

"No such luck," Peter replied. "That was his charming daughter on the phone just now. He's on his way to the office and she's coming around to see you at the house this evening. She must have heard you were having a party."

Judy sighed profoundly.

"Oh, dear! She'll be sure to spoil it by saying something unkind and hurting somebody's feelings. She always does that. I guess it's a Vincent trait. They're not living on their old place in Farringdon, are they? I thought they sold that."

"They did," said Peter, "and for plenty of cash. No. It's another place. Belonged to Kay's uncle. You remember that swanky estate several miles below Roulsville? Well, that's it. Kay said she'd have to have the crowd down there for a get-together sometime. She seemed to think you would all welcome her with open arms."

"She would!" exclaimed Judy in disgust. "But why is her father coming to see you?"

"It's something about her uncle's will,"

Peter explained. "They're contesting it. Kay said they intended to prove that it was forged. Their lawyer is an old teacher of mine and he wants me to assist him at the trial."

"You're not going to do it, are you?"

"Why not?" he asked. "A young lawyer does need practice and I know very little about wills except what I learned in school. This ought to be good experience."

"I know," Judy replied, her gray eyes narrowing. "But I never trusted Harry Vincent. You mustn't let him make trouble for you, Peter. You remember, he was the one who gave us our house in Farringdon, or rather let us have it rent free until Dad was ready to buy it. But there was a trick in that. The house was haunted."

"It wouldn't surprise me if you still had a midnight visitor or two," Peter returned with a grin. "You've tracked down a few ghosts but you've never gone into the house's history. If it could talk I'll bet it could tell you plenty."

"I suppose it could," Judy agreed. "Poor old house! It's too bad everybody can't forget its past and simply love it, the way I do, because the people I love are living in it. It's like a person who's done wrong——"

"Like Harry Vincent," Peter suggested.

"No, because a house can't help what goes on inside it. A person can."

"Always?"

"I don't know. Honestly, I don't," Judy confessed. "I'm not smart enough to understand the workings of a crook's mind. But surely, Peter, you haven't forgotten that Vine Thompson was murdered in our house."

"Of course I haven't forgotten," he replied. "But what does Vine Thompson's murder have to do with this will?"

"Nothing at all," Judy admitted, "except that she was a fence for a gang of crooks and Harry Vincent was involved somehow. He must have known the house was being used for illegal business. Remember how he paid those men to cart stolen liquor out of the wine cellar? And you can't tell me old Vine worked out that elaborate system of secret tunnels and hiding places all by herself."

"Well, suppose she didn't? That doesn't mean Harry Vincent doesn't deserve legal protection if his brother tries to cheat him out of his property."

"They're all cheats—the whole Vincent tribe," Judy declared. "That's why I'm so afraid of this will. It may be thrilling and all that. But suppose you got mixed up in one of Harry Vincent's crooked schemes. You'll expect him to win the case, of course. Lawyers always expect their side to win.''

''Now look here,'' said Peter, facing her seriously. ''What is a lawyer's job anyway if it isn't trying to see that justice is done? If I can't see an honest reason for contesting this will I won't assist at the trial. Those speeches I heard when I was admitted to the bar and sworn in as an attorney weren't just so many words. Grandma and Grandpa had put me through law school at no small sacrifice, I can tell you, and they weren't educating me to be another lawyer crook.''

''I'll never forget how proud your grandparents looked, Peter, when you placed your hand on the Bible and took the oath.''

''That's what I mean,'' he said. ''Too many lawyers forget that oath and think money is the only thing that counts. They're out to win their cases whether they're right or wrong. Well, I'm not. I won't touch this thing if it's crooked.''

He rose from his chair and his voice sounded loud above the noise of the storm. It was at that moment that Harry Vincent strode in, his umbrella making a river of rain water across the office floor. With him was a florid-faced gentleman whom Judy immediately recognized as Mort Sanders, a well-known criminal lawyer who had often given lectures at the law school Peter used to attend.

"Well, well, my boy!" he boomed. "Quite a place you have here. Quite a place! Did we interrupt something or was that illuminating speech I just heard only for the benefit of your secretary?" He peered at Judy as though she were a freak of some kind and added, "I take it she is your secretary."

"This is Judy Bolton, our local girl detective," Harry Vincent put in with an unnecessary bow.

Judy wanted to slap him, but managed to control her feelings.

"Will you sit down, gentlemen?" she asked in her best professional voice.

Harry Vincent hesitated a moment, taking in the whole office in one appraising glance.

"Not afraid of the varnish on these new chairs?" he asked. "We're pretty wet. All this new furniture came from busting up the real estate racket, I take it. Well now, Peter

Dobbs,'' he continued, moving his chair closer, ''there's another little racket I want busted up. If you're as clever as I think you are you can trump up some charge of fraud and get my family their rightful share of my deceased brother's estate. You were talking about justice. Now there's justice for you!''

Mr. Sanders smiled. He appeared to be smiling most of the time.

'' 'Trump up a charge' is hardly the phrase I would use, Mr. Vincent,'' he said. ''The charge is legitimate enough. Lou Vincent, the testator, was incapable of either writing or signing a will at the time this paper was drawn up.''

''We have witnesses to prove that,'' Harry Vincent declared, pounding his fists on Peter's desk for emphasis. ''Unless Lou was tricked into making over his property to my younger brother, Ned, I feel quite certain he would have remembered Kay and Dickie. He was always very fond of them when they were youngsters. Dickie was his favorite and he expected great things of him. What I'm getting at is, he wouldn't have left them out of his will unless that double-crossing younger brother of mine had forged his signature.''

Peter considered all this thoughtfully.

"I take it, then, that the paper was drawn up shortly before Lou's death?"

"The day before, to be exact," the lawyer replied.

"That does change the color of things," said Peter with a low whistle. "But, before I decide, I'd like to see this will for myself and clear up a few questions."

"It's filed in the court house at Farringdon," Mr. Sanders told him. "You're welcome to go in and look it over. Settlement has been somewhat delayed. But we won't go into that," he added quickly. "The trial comes up within a week and, in the meantime, I need a young, clever lawyer to scout around and find new evidence. You might go up to the furniture factory and get whatever records they have of the accident. Lou Vincent was burned with some inflammable furniture polish shortly before he died. Keep anything with his signature on it. Your secretary can help you by hunting through her own house——"

"My house!" Judy exclaimed. "How could there possibly be anything there?"

"I only asked you to look," Mr. Sanders replied and, before he could say more, Harry Vincent hurriedly rose to go. A cold blast of air swept through the office door as the two men departed.

"That wind feels good!" Judy remarked. "The air in here was getting a little stale."

"I'll say it was! Well, Judy, how about it? If we start home now we may reach Farringdon before the county offices close. Before I decide a thing about this case I intend to have a good look at Lou Vincent's will."

"There is something mysterious about it then?"

"Something mighty mysterious," Peter declared. "Lou Vincent, as I remember it, died six or seven years ago. I'll have to ask your brother Horace to look up the details of his death in the old newspaper files. This property should have been distributed years ago. Doesn't it look a bit odd to you?"

She nodded, wishing she understood as much about law as Peter did. She pulled the cover over her typewriter and put her desk in order still wondering why on earth Harry Vincent had come to Peter, of all people. She and Peter, with the help of Horace's daring newspaper articles, had exposed his dishonesty once before and prevented him from becoming Mayor of Farringdon.

"Ready?" asked Peter, sliding her jacket off its hanger on the rack by her desk and holding it for her. "Not much warmth in this," he remarked dubiously.

Judy buttoned it closely.

"Can you see to drive?" she asked as he opened the door. The rain was coming down in sheets.

"I can try," he told her. "It isn't letting up and it may get worse if we wait any longer. Come on, Judy. The car's still there. Let's run for it."

Taking her hand, the two of them dashed out into the storm.

CHAPTER II

It was thirty miles from Roulsville, where the office was, to Judy's home in Farringdon, but she never minded the long trip. It gave her so much more time to discuss things with Peter. It seemed they were always working out some mystery.

Peter kept his car in half of Dr. Bolton's garage and every day he called for Judy and took her home. He knew the road well enough to drive it blindfolded. Or so he said. Judy had her doubts. It was pouring when they made their dash for the car and now they were crawling along unable to see anything but the winking taillight of the car ahead. Everything else was shrouded in blinding rain.

"It makes the road almost as mysterious as Lou Vincent's will," Judy remarked as she turned up the collar of her jacket to keep out the rain that sifted in through the car windows. Peter had the left window open only a crack to prevent the glass from misting over inside. Both windshield wipers were going—*slip! slip!* But through the two half moons of clear glass it was impossible to see anything but rain.

"We'll have another flood if this keeps up," Peter said grimly as he bent over the steering wheel. "But, thank the Lord, there's no dam to break this time. At any rate, no dam above the town. It sort of makes you remember though, doesn't it, Judy?"

She nodded. There was plenty to remember. A storm like this had descended upon Roulsville once before and washed out the dam and flooded the town. Judy had suspected the dam was about to give way and her brother, through an odd mistake, had warned the people in time, but their homes had been swept away like so many cardboard boxes—Judy's and Peter's along with the rest. Three pieces of broken concrete still stood at the head of the valley as a grim reminder of the flood. But Roulsville was no longer a "ghost town." With the help of Arthur Farringdon-Pett, the young architect and building engineer, it was soon rebuilt and Peter became the town's first lawyer. Everything in Roulsville was new now. The buildings were new. The streets were new. To Judy's great delight, one of them was named Judy Lane after her. It was on this street that Peter had built his office. It crossed the valley and joined the main highway just as the road turned up Dry Brook Hollow.

Roulsville Run, the river that ran through the little town, was now a muddy, racing torrent. Just above the broken dam where Dry Brook flowed into it, the waters from the two streams had spread themselves clear across the road. Peter had to turn left on a hill road that was seldom used but which appeared to be well cemented and in good condition. A state trooper in rain hat and high boots was stationed at the intersection to direct traffic.

"Take it easy on the detour, brother," he called out. "This road joins the main highway a mile or so along."

"Thank you, sir!" Peter shouted back at him as his car churned through the muddy water. "Boy! We ought to be in a boat. I don't like detours," he added, turning to Judy. "We may run into trouble."

"Do you still think we'll get to Farringdon by five o'clock?" she asked anxiously.

"Not a chance of it," he answered, "but perhaps you can find out something about the will from Kay at your party this evening. I'll get you home in time for that at any rate.''

''For once I'm glad she's coming,'' Judy said. ''I had hoped to have a regular get-together of all the girls in our crowd but I'm afraid there won't be much of a gathering now that it's raining so hard. I made a cake and it turned out beautifully, for a wonder. That reminds me, Peter, I'm hungry.''

''I could use some food myself,'' he admitted, slowing down the car to a snail's crawl. Although it was still daytime the sky had grown quite dark. Even the white cement road was now hardly visible. The rain was like a curtain around the car, shutting out everything.

''I can't see,'' Peter complained.

Judy wiped the inside of the windshield furiously with a piece of paper towel.

''There! Is that better?''

''A little. But it's still slow going. This storm is the worst I've ever attempted to drive through. I could make it all right on the main road, but an unexpected turn on this detour might send us into kingdom come.''

''That red taillight is still ahead of us,'' Judy told him hopefully. ''I guess we'll be all right if we just follow it.''

"It's risky. But I'll chance it. At any rate, it's level country now. We can't do worse than drive into somebody's field."

"It's all woods through here," Judy observed. The rain had let up a little so that she could see the dripping trees. "Look, Peter! It's like an archway."

Tall maples, heavy with rain, nearly met overhead. Some of the weighted branches scraped the top of the car as Peter drove under them. A few limbs were down and in one place a large rock had slipped into the road. Peter had to steer carefully around it.

"We should come to the end of this detour soon," he remarked. "The speedometer isn't working, but we've certainly gone more than a mile."

"We may have passed the place where we were supposed to turn back on the main road and missed seeing it in the rain. Have you any idea where we are?" Judy asked.

Peter scanned the landscape. The unfamiliar road stretched ahead. Not a house was in sight. The car ahead must have picked up speed or turned off the detour for they were no longer following it. Rivers of rain ran along either side of the pavement. Presently they came to a patch of cleared ground that looked as though it might be a part of somebody's farm.

"I don't recognize a thing," Peter admitted. "But we'll only be losing time if we turn back now. This road is bound to come out somewhere."

"It's paved," Judy agreed, "and that's something. Zowie! Here comes the rain again!"

It slapped the windshield as though a hose had been turned suddenly against it. The car crawled again but this time there were no lights to follow. They came to a fork in the road and Peter turned just in time to avoid hitting somebody's mail box. Judy saw the sign PAVEMENT ENDS too late to call it to his attention. The car had already slipped into a sea of mud.

"Now we are stuck!" exclaimed Peter as the wheels spun. Soon the engine died and Judy could feel the car settling. She gave Peter a look of blank dismay.

"We can't stay here!" she cried. "I had a million things to do at home and Mother will be so worried. She'll think something awful has happened if I'm not home for the party. Kay may think I stayed out on purpose because she was coming. This would be an awful time to have her think that, Peter. What shall we do?"

"I might try jacking up the car wheels but the chances are it wouldn't help much. We're in this mud clear to the hubs."

Judy lowered her window and poked her head out into the rain, attempting to see.

"There's a dark blur out there. It looks like a building," she announced. "Maybe it's a farmhouse and the farmer can pull us out with his horses."

"We can try it anyhow," Peter agreed. "But you'd better stay in the car, Judy. You can't wade through this mud."

"Stay here and let you have an adventure by yourself!" she cried. "Indeed I won't. Mud and rain won't hurt me. I've been wet before."

"Not as wet as you're going to be this time," Peter warned her, opening the car door and lifting her over the muddy road.

"There you are!" he said grimly. "You asked for it."

"I certainly did," she replied, laughing at him through the downpour. "Did you ever hear of Little Miss Rain-in-the-Face? Just now that name fits me."

It was still pouring and the cold drops soon wet both Judy and Peter to the skin. Hand in hand, they ran along the soggy ground toward

the dark blur that Judy had called a building.
It didn't look so much like a farm house now.
There was no barn anywhere near it, only an
orchard of twisted trees and the house—black
against the gray sky. Judy blinked the rain
from her eyelashes to see it more clearly.

"Talk about our house being haunted!"

"It's probably empty," Peter said as they
came nearer.

The house had round windows in the gable
ends nearly like the round windows in the twin
peaks of Judy's own house. All the other
windows were tightly shuttered. The weather-
beaten siding had once been painted but now it
was black as ink. A mass of tangled vines grew
over the latticed porch. Judy had never seen a
more dismal looking place. Peter was right,
she decided, nobody could possibly live there.

"If we weren't drenched already," she said,
"I'd suggest going back to the car."

Peter began blaming himself for everything.

"Only a fool would have taken a girl out in
this storm. Judy! You're shivering!"

"I'm not cold," she assured him between
chattering teeth. But in the next breath she
suggested that perhaps they could find a stove
in the kitchen and build a fire.

"That's a thought," Peter agreed, quickening his steps. Judy ran along beside him, keeping pace. Her shoes oozed water at every step. Suddenly she pointed out a faint glimmer of light through the shutters of the closed house. At first it appeared in one of the upper windows. Then it seemed to move down a stairway, shine for a moment in a lower window and then disappear in the cellar.

"Someone must be carrying a lamp," Judy said, clutching Peter's wet coat sleeve. "But why would anybody take a lamp down cellar and then blow it out? Now if it had been moving in the other direction I could understand it. You can imagine a person wanting to be upstairs in the dark to lie down or something—but not down cellar."

"It is odd. Gosh! I don't like the looks of this place," Peter said. I'd swear it was empty if we hadn't seen that ghostly light. There it is again and, sure enough, it's in the cellar!"

Judy shivered. It reminded her of more than one past adventure—the seven clues she had found in her own cellar, a terrifying night locked in with the Chinaman's spooks and the mysterious shadow she had seen in the cellar of a little house on upper Grove Street.

"There's one thing about it," she observed hopefully as they came up onto the porch, "we've explained all the other cellar mysteries. None of them were half as spooky as they seemed and this one can't be either. I'd rather like to have a look around."

"It's dry inside and that's something."

"It is indeed," Judy agreed. "I feel as though I'd been dipped in a river. If ever I do get home I intend to put on my warmest velvet. This may be summer but it certainly doesn't feel like it. Oooo! What's that?"

"I didn't hear anything."

"I did," Judy declared. "But it may have been only the wind in those apple trees back of the house. It sounded like somebody knocking on the inside of the door."

"People don't knock on the inside of doors."

"Ghosts do," Judy stated in a knowing voice. "That is, if they're trying to get out. I ought to be able to tell. We've had enough adventures with them."

"But not any real ones," Peter reminded her.

"That's just it," she answered sadly. "They were all fakes. It's fun showing them up, of course, but if there were such things as ghosts and if I should ever meet one——"

"I know," Peter interrupted. "You've told me before. You'd walk right up to it and say, 'How do you do, Mr. Ghost,' and in no time at all you and the ghost would be just like that."

He exhibited his thumb and finger, pressed closely together. Meanwhile Judy had her ear at the door. There was a distinct tapping sound inside. It couldn't be caused by the wind.

"Listen!" she said.

Peter heard it too but tried to make light of it.

"You were the one who said 'there's something so comforting about the tapping——' "

"Of the typewriter keys," she finished. "But that's not a typewriter and there's nothing comforting about it. Someone—or something—is rapping on the walls of that house asking to be let out."

"The door must be locked from the outside then. Don't suppose there's any use ringing the bell."

Nevertheless, he rang it. The bell was an old-fashioned affair that turned sideways like a handle. It gave back an unearthly buzzing sound and immediately the rappings ceased.

They waited, breathless, while the wind whistled and the rain beat against the blackened siding. There was no other sound.

"Guess there's nobody there," Peter said at last.

"But there must be," Judy insisted. "Some-one was rapping. And that light didn't travel around by itself either. Someone was carrying it. Let me try the bell."

She gave it a long, hard turn and then listened.

Z-z-z-z-zing! The echo sounded weirdly through the walls.

"Even a ghost would hear that," declared Peter.

"But would a ghost answer it?" Judy joked back at him. "I've heard that ghosts don't need doors. They walk right through them. So it mustn't be a ghost in the house," she added more seriously. "It must be something that could be imprisoned."

"With the lock broken?"

"My goodness! So it is." Judy stood holding the knob that had come off in her hand when she attempted to turn it. Every screw had been taken out of the lock. She braced herself against the panels and, before she could catch her breath from the first hard push, the heavy door swung to. Judy and Peter were now standing inside the mysterious house.

CHAPTER III

"Why, it's built like our house!" exclaimed Judy, peering through the hallway to the stairs beyond. "See! It has the same big hall with stairs at the back and rooms to the right and left. The radio should be about here." She indicated a spot near the right-hand wall. "And this room should be Dad's reception room with his office next and then another door——"

She turned the knob to the door that opened to the left of the hall. It refused to budge.

"Oh, dear! It's locked. But the right hand door is open anyway," she added cheerfully, seeing that it had been left ajar. "This should be the living room. Let's see what's there."

"Here, take my flashlight."

Peter pressed it into her hand and she directed its round beam of light into what she thought would be an empty room.

"Help!" she exclaimed, nearly dropping the flashlight.

24

"Am I seeing things," asked Peter, "or is that white-faced object really there?"

"It's there all right." Judy took a step nearer the apparition and then began to giggle. "My goodness! What a start it gave me. But look, Peter, it's only a statue with a white cover to keep off the dust."

"Lord Byron! Well, old fellow," Peter told the statue, "it looks as though you'd be our host until the rain lets up."

His joking manner cheered Judy, although she was still shivering. Playing the flashlight in all four corners of the room, she saw that it was anything but empty. Tables, chairs, even pictures seemed to peer out at her from underneath white covers. The air was that of a place that had long been closed.

"The people have simply gone off and left their things," she announced. "But wouldn't this house be grand for playing hide-and-seek?"

"Simply grand," agreed Peter, stubbing his toe on a claw that held a glass ball in its grip. The claw proved to be only one of the four legs of a piano stool, covered like everything else. The piano was beside it. Judy touched one of the keys and then wished she hadn't. Every noise they made had a hollow echo.

"This furniture actually seems alive," remarked Judy as they groped about. "Honestly, don't you feel as though it's watching us? Look at this chair with lions carved on the arms! Our host certainly has queer taste in furniture."

"Our mysterious host," said Peter ominously.

He was teasing her, she knew. Peter loved to tease. It made the place seem less spooky when they joked about it. But Judy couldn't help thinking that almost anything might be hidden underneath those ghostly covers. She lifted a few of them and peeped cautiously underneath only to find a large red vase, a pair of silver candelabra tarnished to a greenish black and an old-fashioned lamp with a round china globe.

"I should say some of these things were antiques and quite valuable," Peter remarked as they uncovered more and more quaint pieces.

"If that's so," Judy returned in a puzzled voice, "why would they be stored away in a shabby old house that isn't even locked?"

"It was locked," Peter said, "until somebody removed those screws."

Judy didn't like the way he said *somebody*.

An alarming thought suddenly came to her.

"Maybe we've interrupted a robbery!"

"That's just what I was thinking," Peter told her, "and, if we have, the robbers are still pretty close at hand."

"Down cellar!" Judy's voice was excited. "That's where the light went. We might lock the cellar door and trap them."

"We might," Peter agreed, "except that we're not sure there's anybody down there."

"Couldn't we look?"

"I'm game if you are. But it may be dangerous."

"We've done dangerous things before," said Judy, "and we're still here to tell the story——"

She broke off suddenly, losing some of her courage as a clock underneath one of the white covers gave forth a loud *dong!*

"Half past six," said Peter, comparing it with his watch. "Somebody must have been here to wind it."

Judy agreed. "But burglars wouldn't take the trouble to wind a clock."

Peter, still holding to the burglar theory, continued searching around for the entrance to the cellar. For a moment Judy lost sight of him and the covered furniture and that ghostly clock, still ticking under its sheet, seemed more frightening than ever. She even fancied one of the white covers moved a little. Then Peter poked his head around a doorway and announced:

"I've found the kitchen."

Without pausing to investigate, Judy made a bee-line for it. Coming into that cheerful kitchen after the gloom of the closed rooms she had just left was like escaping from a dungeon. Nothing was covered in the kitchen and Peter had found a lamp. It cast a warm red glow about the room and revealed a huge iron cook stove with wood piled in a box beside it, a chimney cupboard filled with kitchen utensils and supplies and a rather impressive white pine cabinet. Beyond were two doors, side by side.

"If this house really is a twin to ours," Judy said, "one of those doors should lead to the cellar."

"This one's locked."

"But the other one would be the cellar door . . . and look! Oh, Peter! Just *look!* I didn't see it before but over there—" She pointed excitedly to the wall just beside the door through which they had entered the kitchen. "Is it really what I think it is—a telephone?"

"It certainly is." Peter's blue eyes shone. "I declare! This is a find. We can use it if it's connected and if the line isn't down from the storm."

He tried it and, after a few moments, Judy was surprised to hear his voice speaking to someone in the Roulsville garage.

"Yes, we're stuck here. Must have forgotten to turn off the detour onto the main road again. Couldn't see for the rain. Yes. It's right where the pavement ends. Slipped into the mud. That's right. Think you can find it? Sure we'll wait. No. Not in the car. We'll watch for you through the window. We found shelter in somebody's empty house."

"I hope it is empty," said Judy as Peter hung up the receiver. "That light didn't go downstairs by itself, you know, and why would the telephone be connected if there were nobody around to use it?"

Peter heaved a long sigh. "Anyway," he said, "we'll feel a little safer exploring the cellar."

He opened the door and Judy saw a long flight of whitewashed stairs leading down into the blackness below. It smelled earthy and cold.

"Shall I go first?" she asked, but not in her usual eager voice.

"No, I'd better. Watch out for this broken step," Peter cautioned her as he began descending.

"I can't see it," she complained. "Ouch! I've caught my heel. I guess I'd better go first and hold the flashlight. You make such a big shadow."

"Are you all right?" he asked anxiously.

"All but my heel. It came off. The shoes were soaked to pieces anyway and I'm getting on well enough in my stockings."

Her voice was reassuring, but the cellar floor was cold to step on. It was far from wise, she knew, to come down here almost barefoot and soaked to the skin. But she had to see. Playing the flashlight in every corner of the musty cellar, she advanced cautiously. A moth fluttered before the light and, farther on, a cobweb brushed her face. But there was nothing really frightening. The cellar was big and cold and empty. She crossed the entire length of it to the back wall. Suddenly Peter stopped and held her back with his hand.

"What is it?" she questioned in a whisper.

"A row of stone crocks, as far as I can make

out." He wrinkled his nose. "Smell them? Dill pickles!"

"We weren't looking for pickles," she scolded. "We were looking for robbers. See that tin lamp on the shelf! That's the one that must have been burning." She felt of the glass chimney. "It is!" she exclaimed. "It's still a little warm. The robbers must have escaped."

"Not a very thorough job of robbery, if you ask me," grinned Peter. "Look at those shelves filled with canned peaches and raspberry jam!"

Judy glanced at him, taking in the whole situation.

"You're not afraid, Peter Dobbs, and neither am I," she said. "There's not a soul in the place. But there is something to eat and I'm starved as well as half frozen. I really think, if we left a dollar somewhere to pay for it, we might build a fire and make ourselves a little supper."

"Agreed," said Peter. "It sounds to me like a fine idea. But suppose there isn't any bread to go with the jam!"

"I can make biscuits," Judy declared. "There's flour and baking powder. I saw it in the kitchen cabinet as we came down."

"Judy, you're a wonder!" Peter's voice was

enthusiastic. "We can't leave here until the garage men arrive anyway. I'll start the fire."

There was plenty of wood in the wood box. A little of the kerosene from the tin lamp they had found down cellar urged their fire to a quick start and soon the kitchen was quite warm and cozy. Judy toasted her toes for a minute and then set about the task of getting supper. There were dishes in the chimney cupboard— some of them real willow-ware. She found running water at the sink and washed two cups. To her great delight, there was also a container filled with tea. She hummed a little tune as she measured it out.

> "Just tea for two
> And two for tea;
> Just me for you
> And you for me——"

"Do you mean that, Judy?" asked Peter as he fussed with the fire.

"Oh, I was just singing," she replied carelessly. "It makes the place more homelike."

"And you're the girl who always said you couldn't carry a tune?"

"Can I, Peter?" This time there was real pleasure in her voice.

"You have all sorts of undiscovered talents, my dear, and not the least of them is biscuits."

"Save your praise until they're finished," she warned him. "They may be hard as bullets. We may even be obliged to use them as such if the owner of this cheerful little cottage decides to make a sudden attack. By the way, Peter, while I'm stirring up the biscuits, I wish you'd call Mother and tell her I'm safe——"

"Are you?"

"As safe as I ever am," she retorted. "Tell her Honey will have to entertain the company until I get there and—and if Kay Vincent comes she'll have to shut Blackberry in my room. Kay hates cats—and especially Blackberry."

"Anything else?"

"Just don't let her worry. You ought to call your grandparents too. Are they alone?"

"Never, when they're together. I'll take care of everything," Peter promised as he walked over to the telephone. This time, however, the line was completely dead.

"Down from the storm! I should have known it. We can thank our lucky stars we called the garage in time."

"I hope they hurry," Judy said with an apprehensive look toward the dim room beyond.

"I guess I'm getting nervous. I keep imagining someone is hiding under those white covers."

Quietly but firmly, Peter closed the door. "There! How's that for you? There's nobody hiding in the kitchen."

"I guess you think I'm a goose," Judy murmured, returning to the stove to look at her biscuits. They were a beautiful golden brown and as light and fluffy as so many feathers. She popped them out of the oven and turned them out in a deep bowl. The whole room was filled with the odor of hot biscuits.

"I'd like to see anybody human that could resist these," said Peter, helping himself.

Judy filled two glasses.

"Shall we drink to our mysterious host? This is grapefruit juice," she explained. "I found it in a can. Dad says it's good to keep people from catching cold. If so, we'll both need it."

"Wait a minute!" said Peter, his voice tense. "Before we drink to him, hadn't we better see who he is?"

"What do you mean?" Judy began. Then she stopped, speechless. The door Peter had just closed was opening, inch by inch, as they stared in horrified fascination.

CHAPTER IV

THE GIRL WHO HAD SEEN A GHOST

"Who's there?" demanded Peter in a gruff voice wholly unlike his own.

He sprang toward the door, flung it all the way open and faced the blackness of the empty room. Now that it was totally dark, the white sheets stood out like so many tombstones. But there was nobody in sight.

"You were right," he said, turning grimly to Judy. "This is a grand place for playing hide-and-seek."

"We're the intruders," Judy reminded him. "No doubt our host merely looked in to see who we were."

"If he looks again I mean to do some looking myself. No human being is able to make himself quite invisible."

"Now Peter," Judy said, placing her hand on his arm and guiding him back to his chair, "just take this in your stride. We were going to drink to him, you know."

"Okay!" said Peter, raising his glass.

"Here's to our host,
A blooming ghost."

Judy touched her glass to his and was just about to drink the refreshing grapefruit juice when a voice behind her said:

"May I drink with you?"

Whirling in her chair, Judy faced the open door to the room beyond. There, outlined against the darkness behind her, stood a girl with the blackest hair and the bluest eyes Judy had ever seen. She had a white sheet draped around her.

"I didn't mean to frighten you," she said.

For a moment neither Judy nor Peter could speak. This didn't seem real. The girl herself was like a china doll with her black hair and her too white face. She wore her hair in a long bob, tied at the top with a small bow of ribbon. She was beautiful in a breath-taking way. Her lips were parted and her eyes were laughing. Behind the heavy lashes Judy could see them sparkle.

"I didn't mean to frighten you," she repeated.

"Then why the sheet?" asked Peter, finding his voice.

"I hid under it," she confessed. "I was frightened too. But I'm not now. I'd really like to drink that toast to our host the ghost . . ."

She stopped and her silvery laugh rang out.

"It sounds funny, doesn't it? I never thought I'd be able to laugh at a ghost but it's so good to have someone alive to laugh with. You didn't expect to find anybody alive in here either, did you? I guess I sort of took you by surprise."

"I should say you did," agreed Judy. "I nearly fainted when you opened that door."

"But *I* didn't open it," the girl said.

"Then who in the world did?"

"Our host, I guess, unless you opened it yourselves."

"But we didn't," Judy insisted. "We just came in here to get dry."

"You see," Peter explained, "my car's stuck in the mud up the road a bit. We took the liberty of borrowing the telephone here and calling the garage in Roulsville for help. Then, since there appeared to be no one at home, we simply helped ourselves to some food."

"We were hungry," Judy added, "but we

left a dollar to pay for it. I hope your folks won't mind.''

''They're not my folks,'' the girl said. ''I don't live here. Truly I don't. I'm indebted to our host as much as you are.''

''Then who is he?'' asked Peter, pouring out a third glass of grapefruit juice into a heavy, cut-glass goblet he had found in the chimney cupboard.

The girl shrugged her shoulders. ''How should I know? Who are you, for that matter? There's quite as much for you to explain as there is for me.''

Judy looked at her, eyes narrowed. If she didn't know whose house it was, how on earth did she happen to be there? She had dropped the sheet now and stood there in a simple, long-waisted dress that was a little soiled and horribly out of style. Her shoes were shabby, but quite dry. She couldn't have come in out of the storm. She must have been there before it started to rain.

''She's right. Let's all introduce ourselves,'' suggested Peter.

''After you, my lord,'' said the girl with the laughing eyes.

''I'll begin. I'm Judy Bolton and the gentleman is Peter Dobbs. I'm his secretary and he's a lawyer——"

The girl laughed aloud.

"I've heard of Judy Bolton. She isn't a secretary. She's a famous girl detective. You are just trying to fool me. And you're not a lawyer," she added, turning to Peter. "How could a boy like you convince a jury of anything?"

Peter gave it up.

"I'm sure I don't know," he replied, pulling up a chair. "Here, have a biscuit. You might as well sit down with us and make yourself at home."

"You do live here then," the girl said with conviction, and sat down. She broke her biscuit thoughtfully and spread it lavishly with jam. Then she raised her head and looked up, and her eyes weren't laughing as she asked her next question:

"Did you see the ghost too?"

"You mean that thing in the hall? That was only a statue——"

"No," she interrupted. "I mean the real ghost. Everybody knows this house is still haunted."

"Everybody? I didn't."

The girl's bell-like laughter rang out once more.

"Now you are fooling me," she said.

"No, really I didn't know it," Judy declared. "It's queer too. I usually hear such things. My brother's a reporter and he never passes up a haunted house story. I've given him several." She glanced at Peter. "Maybe we can give him another. Were you down cellar just now?" she asked the girl. "Were you, by any chance, carrying a lamp?"

"I blew it out," she said, "when I heard you. I thought you were the ghosts——"

"Do we look as bad as all that?"

"But I hadn't seen you then," she protested. "I didn't dare look. I just blew out the lamp and ran up here and hid again. It wasn't until the door opened and I saw your faces that I knew you were real."

"We're real all right," Judy assured her, "but I still don't understand this ghost business —that door opening and all. It seems as though I would have heard about it if there were another haunted house this near Farringdon."

"Another? What do you mean? Is there one already?"

"Ours," Judy said. "But, of course, not

really.   There aren't any such things as ghosts——"

"You may think not," the girl interrupted. "Your folks are living. Well, mine are all dead —everyone in the world I care about. I didn't believe in ghosts either until—until—" She broke off. "But I can't tell you. You'd laugh and this is one thing that isn't funny."

"We won't laugh, will we, Peter? Really, we won't," Judy promised. "We've been here long enough to know it isn't funny and, if we can, we'd like to help you."

"Do you mean that? Then tell me about your house. Why did they think it was haunted?"

"Oh, people heard noises and saw white things in the windows and there were the usual rappings and moanings and screechings. But the real reason," said Judy, pausing a moment for effect, "was because a woman had been murdered there. Her name was Vine Thompson and nobody felt very bad about her being gone, I guess, unless it was the people who profited from her business. She was a fence for a gang of robbers and one of them shot her. After her death there were all sorts of spooky stories about how she came back and warned people away from the house——"

"Do you think she really did come back? Dead people can, you know."

"I've never believed that," Judy said.

"I wish I didn't." There wasn't a trace of laughter left in the girl's face. "I wouldn't be half so frightened if I didn't believe in ghosts. I never used to believe in them but when I keep on seeing them I just can't help it. They've never tried to hurt me or anything and I keep telling myself there's nothing to be afraid of once you're used to them. That's why you aren't afraid. You're used to seeing ghosts."

"But they weren't real," Judy insisted. "Peter and my brother and all my friends helped me explain things, ghost by ghost, if you follow me——"

"I do. And you explained them all?"

"Every one," said Judy.

"That's how she got all the publicity. That's why you thought she was a famous girl detective," Peter put in. "Well, she is, but she's also my secretary and everything she's telling you is true."

"But she didn't explain this ghost," the girl protested.

"What ghost?" asked Judy.

"The one I'm telling you about. The one I saw.

"My dear little girl," said Peter. "Either you're trying to frighten us or you're scared to death yourself. Let's change the subject. Will you have another biscuit?"

"There aren't any more."

"True!" sighed Peter. "We've eaten them all. You see how silly all these ghost stories are. They didn't even affect our appetites."

"They aren't silly!" cried the girl, almost in tears. "Ghosts aren't silly and they aren't fakes and they aren't funny either. They're awfully sad. They don't see you at all. They look right through you to something else beyond. Everything is probably very beautiful to ghosts."

Judy's eyes met Peter's. Certainly this strange child had seen something. Hers wasn't a silly, superstitious fear, but a positive belief because of something she had seen.

"I thought I was dreaming at first," she went on, "I had to pinch myself several times. It still makes me feel queer to think I'm here and they're—somewhere else."

"Did you ever speak to one of them?" asked Peter with a meaning look at Judy. He remembered a time when she had told him that she spoke to a ghost and told it to hush *and it did.*

"I couldn't speak," the girl said. "I was all choked up—like I am now. I tried so hard to be brave. I'd heard about you, Judy, and you were brave. Even when all the girls in school hated you, you kept on being brave and trying to find out things. I tried to be that way too. I've never told a soul about it before. I don't know why I'm telling you."

"It's best to have it out," Peter said gently. "You ought not to be here alone."

"I know it!" she sobbed, breaking down at last. "I ought not to have come here in the first place. But now that I'm here, Judy, why can't you believe me and treat me like a friend and let me stay?"

"But I can't let you stay in somebody else's house. We'll be going in a minute and your folks, whoever they are, will be worrying about you. Couldn't we take you home?"

The girl looked up and her heavy lashes were wet with tears.

"Are you really going?" she questioned.

"Just as soon as the garage men get here," Judy replied. "Please let us take you home. There'll be plenty of room in the car and I'm sure the worst of the storm is over——"

"You can't take me home," the girl sobbed.

"There isn't anywhere for me to go unless you want to take me to your house."

Taken by surprise, Judy hardly knew how to answer. They had found a strange girl in an apparently empty house. They had no idea who she was or how she got there. The only thing they were sure of was that she thought she had seen a ghost.

"I wish you'd tell me who you are," Judy said at last. "It might help me to decide."

"You can call me Sally."

There was a noise outside and the girl they could call Sally suddenly ran to the window.

"There's the car you telephoned for!" she cried. "It's got a pulley thing on the back and the man is all ready to hook it to your car. I can see by his lantern. Please let me go home with you. I'll explain everything in the morning if you'll just let me stay in your house one night."

CHAPTER V

JUST as they were about to leave the house Judy was seized with a wild desire to explore.

"We haven't explained the door opening or the ghost Sally thinks she saw or anything," she said. "And here we are planning to just walk off and leave a whole house full of mysteries."

"What else can we do?" Peter asked logically. "We're expected at home and the garage men are already pulling the car out and Sally's promised that she will explain herself in the morning. Besides, we've been in every room in the house except the one that's locked——"

"Or the two," Judy amended. "If the house is like ours——"

"Is it?" Sally interrupted. "I thought it must be. Both of them are haunted."

"I was going to say, if the house is like ours there are two rooms at the left of the hall. They correspond to Dad's reception room and his office. One opens into the hall and the other into

46

the kitchen. It's quite possible our host is in there this very minute. Let's knock."

"I did knock," Sally declared. "I banged and thumped all over the place. You must have heard me."

"That knocking on the inside of the door? Then that was you? But it couldn't have been," he added. "You said you were in the cellar when we came up on the porch."

"But I was knocking down there too."

"Knocking in the cellar of an empty house!" he exclaimed. "No wonder you thought the place was haunted. What on earth made you do it?"

"Just looking for things," she replied. "You're taking me, aren't you?"

"We can't very well leave you," laughed Judy, "but don't forget, I'm counting on you to explain a lot of things. I rather suspect you of being a princess in disguise."

"I'm in disguise all right," said the girl as she pulled a dark cloak over her shabby dress. The cloak had been flung over a chair as though she had removed it hastily and made for her hiding place. "I'm all ready," she announced.

"Better turn up your collar. It's still raining," Peter told her.

On sudden impulse, Judy turned and rapped on the locked door.

"Thanks—for the hospitality—if there's anybody in there!" she called. "We washed up our dishes and left a dollar in the kitchen. 'Bye-eee!"

Peter was pulling her along, half-laughing.

"It's silly talking to ghosts," said Sally with a shiver.

"I wish I knew what was in there," said Judy regretfully as she followed Peter through the wet meadow back to the car. He had her hand and she held fast to Sally's. The rain was now only a fine mist, but the wind howled and whistled.

"It's blowing up for a hurricane," said Peter. "I don't like wind one bit better than I do rain. A tree down across the road could block a car as badly as this mud hole ever did, to say nothing of what might happen if a tree should fall and pin us under it——"

"Mr. Gloom!" scolded Judy. "Your car's out. What more do you want? Look at the poor thing! We'll have to name it Piggsy after the mud bath it's had."

Judy could see the car distinctly in the glow from the garage men's lanterns. They had pulled it out bodily and set it upon the pavement but it was still spattered and streaked with mud. She could also see the mail box, white above its dark post, just where the pavement ended.

Why hadn't she thought to look before? There was a name on the mail box! In dim capitals, almost worn off by age, she made out the final letters of the name, Burlingame, and concluded that such a family must have lived in the shuttered house. They might still live there! Sally might even be their daughter! She had insisted that everyone she cared about was dead, but somebody must have taken care of her until today. Judy began to have all sorts of misgivings. She certainly didn't intend to help the child run away from her own people.

"There's going to be trouble when we get home," she prophesied.

"What trouble?" asked Sally.

"How am I going to introduce you? People will expect to be told your whole name."

Sally asked, "Couldn't you name me Jones or something?"

Judy shook her head. "That wouldn't do. Jones is too common. How would you like to be called Sally Burlingame?"

To Judy's great disappointment, the name made no impression on Sally.

"It's all right if you think so," she said. "I don't care what you call me."

Judy sighed. It was a good clue. The only trouble with it was that it hadn't worked.

Peter waited only to thank the garage men, adding a substantial tip to their regular charge. The men were nearly as muddy as the car. They directed him back to the main road, explaining that he should have turned off the detour about a mile back.

"Better luck this time," they called good-naturedly as Peter climbed in and started the motor. Judy and Sally cuddled together for warmth. Already the strange girl she had found in the shuttered house seemed like a friend. A mystery, Judy decided, was much nicer if it had another girl in it—like Scottie's problem or the time she had discovered Honey. Selma Brady, too, had figured in a surprising mystery. As they rode home through the wind and rain Judy told Sally about the friends she was likely to meet.

"You'll like Selma Brady. She lives in the next house above ours. She and Tag Hamilton are about your age and fast friends. Scottie is a little older, but you'll like her too. She's another neighbor who lives past what Kay Vincent used to call 'the dividing line.' "

"Tell me about it."

"About what?" asked Judy.

"The dividing line—and Kay Vincent. I'm curious."

"Well," Judy explained, "when we first moved to Farringdon our house was in sort of a run-down condition. It needed painting and the lawn was all grown over with weeds. It looked haunted then, I can tell you. And it was right on what everybody called the dividing line between the nice section and the poor section of Farringdon. Harry Vincent, Kay's father, owned all the houses beyond it and, since only the mill workers lived there, he figured they didn't need to be fixed up or anything. You see, all the Vincents have a queer notion that poor people are different from other human beings. They figure that they're poor because they want to be, I guess. Anyway, according to their ideas, there wasn't any reason for trying to improve conditions. So he just let things go. The workers were underpaid and underfed and all the down-town girls turned up their noses at them. Well, Dad didn't feel that way about it, and neither did I. They were our neighbors and, to tell the truth, they were a great deal more friendly than the down-town crowd. Finally, when the ghosts I told you about were all explained, I had a party and invited them all—down-towners and mill workers both. Irene Lang, one of the mill workers, sang and won their hearts. She's Irene Meredith now. You may have heard her singing on the radio.''

"I have!" exclaimed Sally. "Well, I guess that knocked Kay's pet theory all to splinters.''

"It took more than that. There isn't any dividing line now," Judy told her, "but some of the houses Harry Vincent still owns are in pretty awful shape. The Vincents haven't changed their ideas any. It's just the rest of us. Lois and Lorraine used to feel superior but now they welcome just anybody who's nice, no matter where they live. They'll probably be at the house too. I asked them all in for a party.''

"It's an awful night for it," said Sally. "Suppose nobody comes.''

"Honey'll be there anyway," Judy answered cheerfully. "You'll see why we call her that the minute you meet her. She's Peter's sister and a perfect darling. Selma and Scottie ought to be there too, since they live so near. But I'm not sure about the others.''

Sally was silent for a moment, biting her lip and apparently thinking about something.

"This girl—Kay Vincent. You don't think she'll come, do you?''

"I hardly think so," Judy replied. "She said she would when she talked with Peter over the telephone but that was before it started to rain so hard. Her father came into the office later with his lawyer to ask Peter something about a will—" Judy interrupted herself with a laugh. "I'd almost forgotten that, and yet I thought it was quite a mystery until I met you."

"The will?" questioned Sally. "How could a will be a mystery?"

"It's Lou Vincent's will," Judy explained. "He's been dead a long time and we don't quite understand why the will should come up for settlement this late. You see, Harry Vincent—that's Kay's father—claims his younger brother forged Lou's signature. I didn't understand it very well. But anyway, he's contesting the will and has asked Peter to appear at the trial."

"Peter—this boy here—is on Harry Vincent's side?" she asked, eyes wide.

"He isn't sure yet. He hasn't seen the will. We're both going down to the court house and have a look at it the first thing in the morning."

"Would it be all right if I went with you and looked at the will too?"

"I guess it would. The will is open for public inspection. It couldn't do any harm, could it?" she asked.

Judy appealed to Peter who had been keeping his eyes on the slippery road.

"No harm and not much of any good either. A will," he explained, "is a legal document which would probably be very boring to anyone not directly concerned."

"But I like mysteries," Sally insisted. "I've always wanted to know more about wills and what happens to people's property after they're dead."

"They can't take it with them, that's sure," laughed Judy. "But they do have some rights. That's what lawyers are for—to protect them."

"Then, if you could prove that Lou Vincent signed the will himself and knew what was in it, Kay's family couldn't get the property?"

"That's true," Judy answered slowly, "but Peter's on the other side—or will be," she added, "if he decides to work on the case. He will be trying to prove that Ned Vincent, the younger brother, forged the will."

"Oh, I see," said Sally and for a little while after that they rode through the rain without speaking. Sally's face had turned suddenly very white.

CHAPTER VI

THE SECRET ENTRANCE

"I'M BEGINNING to understand something about law," Sally spoke up presently. "It's something like a game, isn't it? You do anything you can to win?"

She was sitting in the front seat, between Judy and Peter, but now it was to Peter, the young lawyer, that she directed her questions.

"Well, perhaps, but always within reason," he replied. "Naturally, you wouldn't cheat in law any more than you would cheat in a game. You'd present your case as clearly as possible and so would the counsel for the other side. Then it would be up to the judge and the jury, if there is one."

"Isn't there always a jury?" questioned Sally.

"Not in cases like the one we were talking about. There's only the lawyer, his assistants, special guardians for minor children and the judge."

"But that isn't fair," she protested. "There ought to be a jury. Who are these special guardians?"

"Lawyers appointed by the court," he replied. "If the child is over fourteen she can select her own lawyer."

"The lawyer only sees one side of the case, doesn't he?" she asked. "He talks with the person who is contesting the will and doesn't bother about the—the——"

"You mean the beneficiary," Peter supplied. "In this case it's Ned Vincent. I intend to have a talk with him just as soon as possible——"

Sally looked dismayed.

"Can you? Then why can't you find out the real truth from Lou Vincent himself?"

"Because, my dear girl, Lou Vincent is dead."

"But if you can talk to one ghost, why can't you talk to another? Judy talked to a ghost back there in the house. Why couldn't you?"

"Because we're not spiritualists, either of us," Peter replied, trying to be patient. "If you're going to start in on ghosts again, I'd advise you to forget the will altogether——"

"But I can't," she interrupted. "I'm going to meet Kay Vincent and you said you were going to talk about the will. I want to be able to talk too.''

"You'll be able to talk all right," Peter replied with meaning. "Judy, won't you see if you can't interest her in something else? I have to pay attention to the road.''

"I did try to interest her in the party," Judy said. "You want to meet my friends, don't you, Sally? Then I'd suggest that, instead of worrying your head over what you'll talk about, we begin to plan what you're going to wear. You may be a princess in disguise, but even Cinderella didn't go to the ball in her rags.''

"These are awful rags, aren't they?" Sally said, glancing down at the clothes she was wearing.

"I didn't mean that," Judy hastened to explain. "But look at me! Do you think I want to walk into the house in a heel-less shoe. Kay would be scandalized and goodness only knows what the others might say. I'll tell you what we'll do.'' She lowered her voice to almost a whisper in an attempt to interest Sally. "We won't go in the front door at all. We'll tiptoe up the back stairs and change our clothes before we meet a soul. I feel like dressing up after the drenching I've had, and I'm sure I can find something for you."

"Something you've outgrown?"

"Maybe, but it won't be too terribly out of style. You won't mind, will you? You're so much smaller than I am."

"I won't mind. I'm getting quite used to wearing outgrown clothes," Sally said with a sigh. "If I ever have children of my own I hope they're quintuplets and all the same size so there won't be any leftovers."

An older sister, thought Judy. She had given away something without knowing it. But she had never met a girl who could ask as many questions and give as few answers as Sally.

"Are you sure we can get into your house without being seen?" she questioned presently.

"Quite sure," Judy replied. "I've told you a lot about the mysteries I've solved, but there's one thing I didn't tell you. Our house has a secret entrance——"

Sally's eyes widened.

"Does it really? Now I'm sure it was all a mistake."

"What was?"

"Oh, everything," Sally replied. "Us being in the other house and not believing each other.

You didn't belong there any more than I did. But now things are turning out all right," she went on happily. "I don't have to poke around through that scary place any longer and tomorrow I can pay you for everything you've done. I can hardly wait to meet your friends— especially Kay Vincent."

"I think I'll present you to my family first," Judy said, her voice skeptical.

"I'll love that!" cried the invincible Sally. "I've heard so much about them. I'm sure they'll be adorable. Are you really going to call me Sally Burlingame?"

Judy was nonplussed. There was no telling what this strange child would say next.

"Where did you ever find such a funny name?" she went on eagerly. "I think I'll adopt it for my very own."

"I wouldn't," Judy advised her. "It was on the mailbox beside that house where we found you."

"Oh, then somebody named Burlingame must have lived there once. But I don't mind pretending. You have to call me something and I'm beginning to get used to having only ghosts for relatives. Your brother will be scared when we tell him. Judy, I'm dying to meet your brother.

I read in the newspapers how he said he wasn't really the hero of the Roulsville flood because he was scared himself. He was like me. But wasn't it wonderful the way he saved the whole town? His picture was in the paper. He is awfully good-looking, isn't he Judy?"

"Why, I hadn't thought of it. He's just Horace. He doesn't think he's good-looking."

"He wouldn't. He didn't think he was a hero either. I've seen your picture in the paper too," Sally ran on. "I might have recognized you if I had known you had red hair. There was something about Peter too and that young landscape gardener he defended. Peter's really a good lawyer, isn't he? I mean if he works on a case he believes in it and does everything he can to see that his client wins? He wouldn't work on a case with a made-up charge——"

" 'Trumped up,' is the phrase Harry Vincent used," Peter put in, interested in spite of himself.

"I mean," she continued, "suppose he was Kay's guardian, he'd do everything he could to see that she wasn't cheated out of anything that was really hers? Whether he liked Kay or not, he'd just think of what was fair and right?"

"I hope he would," Judy replied, giving Peter a defiant glance.

"Yes, whether I liked Kay or not and I can assure you I do not," Peter said.

"But if she did want you to be her guardian, would she just have to ask you to be?"

"You're running into complications again," laughed Peter. "No, she'd have to go to the court-house and sign a petition. But don't worry, Kay's father will see that she gets all that is coming to her."

"I suppose so," Sally agreed. "It's nice having a father. I've heard about your father too, Judy, and the wonderful work he's doing for the Farringdon hospital. I guess you wouldn't know what to do without him, would you?"

"I do depend on him," Judy admitted. "But you're forgetting my mother. She's a peach too. She's more quiet about it than the rest of us but she's the pillar on which the whole family leans for support—even Dad. Poor Mother! She will be so worried."

"What will she say when she sees me?"

"I haven't the remotest idea. But she expects queer things of me," Judy added more hopefully. "I brought a stranger home once before and now she's my dearest friend."

"I wish I could be your friend."

"My dear girl, you are!" Judy exclaimed

warmly. "Whatever trouble you're in, we'll help you. I rather like your being so mysterious. I've found out from past experience that there's always some fascinating story back of any mystery. Naturally I'm anxious to hear yours but, since you don't want to tell me, I'll just trust you have a good reason for keeping it secret until morning."

"I have," Sally declared and then fell silent.

Peter continued his careful driving. Several times the car skidded and once it almost left the road. Water stood in puddles that glistened and reflected rainbows. The wind grew stronger as they neared Farringdon. It was good to be out of the woods and driving on a smooth, straight highway.

The court-house clock struck nine as they passed it. Only four hours since their adventure began, and so much had happened! It seemed impossible that there was still time for a party.

"This is our street," Judy said as they turned up Grove Street at the courthouse square. "See how pretty it is with the little park in the middle. That house with the turrets is where Lois lives. Doesn't it remind you of a medieval castle?"

"It reminds me of a prison," Sally answered unexpectedly. "Those big houses aren't always as cheerful as they look."

Judy had never thought of it that way. A small house was more cozy.

"Thank goodness! Our house isn't quite that big," she said. "I still help Mother dust on Saturdays."

"May I help while I'm there?"

Judy gave Peter a dismayed glance. How long was the girl expecting to stay?

"Well, here's the house. I see the wind hasn't blown it away," he said.

Sally studied it, her head tilted critically to one side.

"It does look a little like that other house," she said.

"It looked more like it before we had it painted white," Judy told her, "but, I assure you, it won't be that spooky."

"I wouldn't be too positive of that."

"Why, what do you mean?"

"The same ghost—Well, I mean if this house is haunted too, you know, there isn't any reason why he couldn't come here——"

"But I told you——"

"I know, but look at the house now!"

Judy shivered. It was just the storm that made everything appear so out-of-line. The shades were drawn although nearly every window in the house was lighted. Probably the radio was on full blast. It usually was whenever they had a party. The wind howled through the branches of the hollow tree in front of the house, bending it with the weight of the storm. Twigs that had already blown off were picked up again and went skimming along the sidewalk. Peter turned into the driveway.

"Nobody could possibly hear us now," Judy said. "You were right, Peter. It was blowing up for a hurricane."

The garage doors slammed shut before Peter had time to close them. Judy snapped on the light.

"Now for the secret!" she announced, her eyes lighting up. Going in through the tunnel was still an adventure. No matter who had used it in the past—or why, it now belonged to the Boltons. Judy felt a special pride in being able to reveal such a mysterious entrance. She found the iron ring that pulled open the trap door in the floor of the garage. There was another trap door just like it, she explained, in the floor of the cellar.

"How exciting!" cried Sally, hopping up and down and clasping her hands. "May I try it?"

"There aren't any steps—just a ladder," Judy told her. "But it's safe. Go ahead! I'll follow you."

"It wobbles a little," Sally said as she began descending. "It—*oooh!*"

What she had started to say was lost in a splash and a gurgle. It took Judy only a second to realize what had happened. The tunnel was flooded and Sally had fallen in. Peter had already removed his coat and was ready to dive into the black water that now swirled underneath the floor of the garage.

CHAPTER VII

THE EMPTY TIN BOX

"It's all right! Don't follow me!" Sally called out. "I can swim."

"But you don't know the way!"

"Yes, I do! I've found the other trap door already. There! I'm out. Please don't jump into that cold water after me. I'm all right! I'll wait here and you can go in properly through the door."

Her voice was a little shaky but quite determined.

"She's a funny kid all right," Peter said. "But as long as she's safe, there's no reason why we shouldn't do as she asks."

"I suppose not," Judy agreed. "Going in through the tunnel was just another good idea that didn't work. It would have been convenient, to say the least. I'm an awful mess to walk in through the door. If Kay Vincent ever sees me——"

"Hang Kay!" Peter said, taking her hand.

"I'd like to walk in just the way we are and watch the expression on her face."

"We can't! We can't leave Sally alone in the cellar. She's probably scared half to death already. Suppose something happened!"

"What could?"

"Nothing, I suppose, but plenty has happened there in the past. Vine Thompson——"

Peter clapped his hand over Judy's mouth.

"Don't you dare remind poor Sally of that." They were hurrying along toward the house— almost blown along by the wind. Somehow they managed to sneak in through the back door without anybody but Horace seeing them. He made some remark that Judy didn't try to hear. She knew she'd hear plenty of teasing from her brother later but now her immediate concern was for Sally.

"I'll go down," she directed Peter. "You go in there." She motioned toward the living room. "Tell them that I've arrived and that I'll be with them in a minute. You might add that I've brought a guest named Sally Burlingame."

"So that's her name?"

"That's what we'll call her."

"Okay," said Peter. He departed through

the door that went on into the front of the house. As he opened it Blackberry darted through to greet his mistress, rising on his hind legs to be stroked and making his usual welcoming sound which was something between a purr and a meow.

"Good Blackberry," crooned Judy. "Kay Vincent can't be in there or you would have been shut out."

Taking the cat in her arms, she started for the cellar. The light was already on. Sally must have found it.

"Sally!" she called softly. "You're there, aren't you? It's all right to come up. I don't think anybody can see us if we just tiptoe quietly upstairs and change."

The silence that answered her was ominous.

Judy raced downstairs, her thoughts in a whirl of confused self-accusations. "Why didn't I follow her? Why did I ever let her go down into that awful tunnel? Why didn't I look first and see the water? She may be drowned. She may be . . ."

But Sally was none of these terrifying things that Judy's mind pictured. She was only sitting, very dejected-looking, on the edge of the round opening which, when closed, formed the almost

invisible entrance to the cellar. Underneath
her was the ladder, carefully placed. Judy almost fell over it.

"Sally, what on earth? I thought you'd be
waiting in the second cellar. How did you ever
put the ladder up all by yourself and how did
you know where to put it? This opening is almost invisible from the other side."

"I found it. The second cellar was a little
wet . . ."

"Of course. How stupid of us! You might
have been drowned."

"There was no danger of that," Sally assured
her. "It was all quite . . . quite interesting."

"Quite dangerous, if you ask me. Sally,
what's that?"

In the girl's hands was an empty tin box—a
box Judy had never seen before. Sally had put
it quickly behind her back as though she had
been attempting to hide it. Now she placed it
on the floor beside her. Blackberry, always a
curious cat, sniffed at it. Yes, it was quite
empty.

"It's just something I found," Sally explained inadequately. "It's just a box. There
was nothing in it."

"I can see that."

Judy eyed the box inquisitively.

"It looks as though there had been something in it, doesn't it?"

"It certainly does," Judy agreed. "It looks like a strong box, the kind people use to protect valuable papers or large sums of money. It locks, doesn't it?"

"With a padlock. See!" She pointed out the catch where the padlock was supposed to fit. "But I guess it's gone."

"It's gone all right. Sally, where did you find this box?"

"Just around. Is it safe to go upstairs and take off these wet clothes?"

"Don't ask me what's safe any more!" exclaimed Judy, throwing up her hands. "I think, Sally, that you'd better put that box right back where you found it before we leave this cellar."

"But I can't," Sally protested. "I found it in the second cellar, down at the lower end where the water's up to your knees. It's awfully dark and muddy down there. Please, Judy! You wouldn't expect me to go back into that awful hole. Why can't we just leave the box here?"

"I guess we can," Judy agreed reluctantly. "Well, come on, before you discover anything else down here. I never in my life saw such a girl for getting into trouble."

"I'm wetter than you are now," Sally said plaintively, "and dirtier than Peter's car."

"And shivering like a piece of jelly," Judy added. "What you need is a hot bath and some clean, dry clothes. Come along! And don't worry about being seen. I could explain everything by simply saying that you were a mud turtle washed in by the storm."

Dripping water at every step, Sally followed Judy to her room. Blackberry came after them, sniffing their muddy tracks. It was usually the cat and not his mistress who tracked up the stairs.

"I must remember to help clean," Judy was thinking. "Mother's in for enough trouble without mopping up after us."

She left Sally in the bath room with a supply of clean towels and soap while she hunted through her bureau for fresh clothes that would be small enough to fit her. Finally she found a slip she had outgrown and passed it in through the bath room door.

"I'll be out in a minute," Sally called.

"Put your muddy clothes in the hamper," Judy called back, "but leave a little space for mine. They're nearly as bad."

In another five minutes Sally was back in Judy's room, filling it with the delicate odor of the perfumed bath soap she had used. Clad only in the slip, she looked smaller and thinner than ever.

"Throw this blanket over yourself and keep warm until I find the rest of your clothes," Judy told her, tossing her a soft pink and white plaid blanket that had been folded in a triangle at the foot of the bed.

Judy herself had huddled into her bath robe, too chilled to think of clothes until after she had finished with her own hot bath. Just as she was about to depart for the bath room a familiar tapping sounded softly on her bed room door. Judy knew at once it was her mother. She had hoped to have a word with her before she and Sally came downstairs.

"Come in, Mums!" Throwing open the door, she pounced on Mrs. Bolton with one smothering hug. "It's so good to be home!" she cried. "Motherkins, did Peter tell you?"

"About Sally? He said you'd brought her home——"

"Well, here she is! I'm hunting up some clothes for her."

"Of course, dear," Mrs. Bolton agreed. "I'm sure your friends will love to meet her. You'll be disappointed, Judy girl, but Lois and Lorraine couldn't come. Lorraine has a little cold and her folks thought it wouldn't be wise to bring her out in this storm. Arthur might have brought them but he telephoned that his car was stranded somewhere on the road. Kay Vincent was here but had to go out on some errand. She may come in again later."

"I don't believe she will," Judy declared, "not in this hurricane. But it's just as well. I've had enough excitement without trying to cope with Kay."

"I guess I'd just as soon not meet her either," Sally spoke up surprisingly. "I'm beginning to lose a little of my courage."

"You'll like the others," Mrs. Bolton reassured her. "I have a suggestion, Judy. Your new dress—the pale blue one—well, it didn't wash very well. I should have sent it out to the cleaners. You see, it shrank——"

"Are you trying to tell me it will fit Sally?"

"Exactly."

"You angel!" cried Judy. "Here you must have worried yourself almost to pieces over me and yet you come up here with smiles and helpful suggestions and not a word about it. Isn't she a peach of a mother, Sally?"

But the smaller girl's eyes were misty.

"I haven't any mother to worry about me," she said. "I wish I had."

"She's going to tell us her whole story in the morning," said Judy smiling into her mother's eyes. "I'm anxious to hear it. You know how I love mysteries and how, just the other day, I was pining for a new one——"

Mrs. Bolton sighed.

"I remember. It's what I expected. You'll put Sally in the guest room, I suppose?"

"The one where Honey always sleeps when she stays all night? Yes, Mother."

"By the way, that last name, Burlingame, sounds a little familiar," Mrs. Bolton said, "I think it was some friend of your father's and it does seem to me he had a daughter. I'll have to ask him."

"Let me talk to him about it," Judy begged. "There's a lot I haven't told you, Mother. We mustn't any of us try to find out things until morning when Sally is ready to tell us. She's been frightened—and upset. You understand."

"Yes, quite. Peter told me you had rescued her. Well, run along and have your own bath now, Judy dear. Your friends are waiting to meet her."

Sally smoothed out the folds of the blue silk

dress and gave Judy's mother a grateful smile.

"You're both almost too wonderful," she said. "I'm not used to people being kind to me. I hardly know how to repay you now—or how to explain. But Judy, you will believe me, won't you? That box I found was empty. I don't understand it any more than you do. Tomorrow I hope we can find out a great many things."

"I hope so too," Judy agreed, pausing with her arms full of the clean clothes she meant to wear. "Tomorrow we're going down to the courthouse and look at Lou Vincent's will and you're going with us—but not," she reminded her, "until after you've told us your whole story. How do I know we shouldn't be returning you to your folks this very minute?"

"You don't know," Sally answered thoughtfully. "But you're going to be glad you kept me. I may not be able to pay you in money but I'll pay you in other ways. You see, Judy, I have another reason for wanting to go to the courthouse with you. It isn't only because I'd like to see that will."

Judy smiled.

"I rather thought you were in some trouble. But, for the rest of the evening, you are to just forget all about it and simply have a good time."

CHAPTER VIII

A GAME IS INTERRUPTED

WHEN Sally presented herself to Judy's friends a half hour later she was the picture of loveliness. The pale blue set off her eyes with their fringe of dark lashes. A little pair of white sandals Judy had worn only twice just fitted her feet and her hair was brushed to a glossy, blue-black sheen. Judy had changed into a flowered dress of rust and green that was particularly becoming as it matched her own coloring. To look at the two girls, no one would have dreamed that shortly before they had both been drenched to the skin—Judy with rain and Sally with muddy water that had seeped into the secret tunnel underneath the garage and the Bolton's mysterious second cellar.

"I hear you've had another adventure," said Honey, stepping forward with a welcoming smile.

"Yes," replied Judy, "and here she is. Girls, meet Sally Burlingame."

"Not Dr. Burlingame's daughter——" began Marge Hamilton. But her sister Betty stopped her and Tag, as usual, spoke up with the wrong thing.

"Of course not, don't you remember——"

But whatever it was they were supposed to remember, Judy was not to know. Tag was squelched, also as usual, and Selma Brady and Dora Scott—Scottie, for short—then came forward with their greeting.

The girls liked her find. Judy could see that. In a short time everybody was talking and laughing. Peter and Horace joined them. The boys felt welcome—Horace especially so as Sally immediately lionized him. He was the hero she had read about and now she wanted the whole story first-hand. She drank in every word he said in wide-eyed admiration.

Peter, of course, had cleaned up a little and borrowed Horace's dry shoes and socks. He had telephoned his grandparents. Fortunately, the line wasn't down in Farringdon—not yet. Outside the wind shrieked and wailed. It made the fire in the big grate twice as welcome. Cocoa with marshmallows and the cake Judy had made were served in the living room.

"We had sort of a supper," she explained,

"while we were keeping dry in the Burlingame house. We fixed it ourselves. But there wasn't any dessert."

"Not very hospitable of me, was it?" asked Sally, her eyes twinkling. "You know, I'm supposed to be the daughter of the house."

"I think you're fooling us," spoke up Betty Hamilton. "You haven't told us your real name. I'm sure I've seen you somewhere before."

"I was supposed to keep out of sight," said Sally.

"She gets more and more mysterious. She's doing it on purpose to tease us," Horace declared. "There's one thing I like about Judy's mysteries though. They're usually quite pretty."

"Quite pretty!" exclaimed Scottie. "Horace Bolton, you know she's beautiful."

"Striking would be the word," said Peter.

"Breath-taking is more like it," Judy put in. "I'm still trying to catch mine."

"Some people," announced Marge, "win popularity by being clever; others can recite or sing or make up new games to play. But Sally is wiser. She has you all oogle-eyed simply because she knows how to keep a secret."

"What secret?" asked Selma, helping her-self to another marshmallow.

"Don't ask me," Marge replied. "I don't know it either. But believe me, girls, I'm doing my best to think."

"It always was an effort," Betty could not resist adding. And Tag, because her sisters were quarreling with each other and not with her, gave Sally such a smile that she immedi-ately won her heart.

"Please tell us," they coaxed.

But Sally only shook her long, dark bob and smilingly promised that they would all know her secret in the morning.

"You know what happens to secrets when there's a newspaper man around," Horace warned her.

"You cheat!" shrieked his parrot from the cage behind him.

Horace turned on the bird and shook his fist in mock indignation.

"And here I've been priding myself on being the one and only honest newspaper re-porter——"

"Ha! Ha! Ha!" laughed the parrot.

"It's time to cover him," said Judy, throwing a cretonne affair of flowers on a green background over the wire cage. "Horace keeps this awful creature," she explained, "in the fond hope that some day he will shout 'you cheat!' at an honest-to-goodness crook and make him 'fess up."

The wind howled louder while they laughed and talked inside the house. When the cake was nearly finished and the cocoa cups empty someone suggested going home. It was getting along toward midnight.

"But you can't go in this wind," Judy protested.

For a few minutes they all watched the storm from the window. Every tree was bent with the force of the wind and green leaves were swirling down as red and yellow ones do in Autumn. A branch cracked off the hollow tree and skated off the porch roof, playing a strange rat-a-tat on the lattice as it slithered down.

"You're right, Judy," Scottie agreed. "It wouldn't be safe to go now. Can't we start a game or something until this wind quiets down a little?"

Selma Brady had a suggestion.

"Let's play Murder!"

The others crowded around her, wanting to know how to play it. Judy already knew. It was hardly a game she would have chosen for this particular night. The wind and rain made the night black enough without turning out all the lights.

According to the rules of the game, the one chosen secretly by cards or by straws to be "it" had to find his victim in the dark. He seized him by the throat—gently, of course, for it was only in fun—and the victim screamed. That was the signal to turn on the lights and go about the serious business of finding out who committed the crime.

"It sounds like a good game," Betty declared when Selma had finished explaining it. "May I be the detective?"

"You have to leave the room. The detective isn't called in until afterwards. You have to be quite a distance away while the game is going on as you're not supposed to know anything about it except what you find out by asking questions. You could go upstairs or down into the cellar," Judy told her.

"May I be the detective next time?" Sally asked eagerly.

It was agreed. There was time for several games if the wind kept up and they would all take turns being detective. Tag had to mention the fact that it seemed odd to play murder in a house where once— But she got no farther. Tag Hamilton never finished her sentences when Betty and Marge were around to stop her.

The game was exciting to say the least. With the lights out, every sound was magnified. Feet that had been almost noiseless before now thumped and tramped. Whispers, giggles, smothered exclamations issued from behind chairs and sofas where people were hiding. Judy suspected Horace, not Blackberry, of the cat calls they heard. Then the squeal would ring out—sometimes two or three times in order to be heard above the wind.

Everybody wanted to be the murderer. It was fun to grope about in the darkness looking for a victim. Judy wondered how it happened that the crowd had never played this exciting game before. She and Honey had played it quite often at Selma's house with her younger brother and sister and Tag and the delightful Mrs. Brady who hadn't quite grown up herself.

Although, on a less exciting night, Betty would probably have called any game that her little sister played childish, she made a good detective. So did Sally. Later Peter and Horace took turns and were even better. It was quite a trick to ask just the right questions to trap the murderer. Everybody else was supposed to tell the truth but "it" could lie as much as he pleased. Only to the question, "Did you commit this murder?" was he obliged to tell the truth. The first question the detective asked was usually, "Where were you at the time of this crime?" Naturally the murderer would place himself in a spot far removed from the one where the victim was found. But, by questioning the others and by receiving truthful answers, he could usually be cornered.

The night wore on. It was midnight now and still the storm raged. Judy, hiding near the front door, could hear it. But she could also hear something else—the most curious tapping. Tap, tap on the sidewalk and then up the front steps. Suddenly the shrill *ting!* of the door bell sounded through the house.

"I'll answer it," she called. "It's probably Kay. Mother said she might come later, though I hardly expected her at this hour. The rest of you just go on with the game. I'll explain it to her and she can join us."

CHAPTER IX

A TREE FALLS

INSIDE the house everything was perfectly quiet. Nobody answered Judy when she called her directions and she knew why. If the game were to go on uninterrupted there was no reason why anyone should reveal his special hiding-place.

Closing the living room door so that the light shining through could not disturb the players, Judy turned on the hall light. Then she threw open the front door, expecting nothing unusual, and braced her body against the wind that whistled through.

A stranger stood there leaning on his cane. He was tall, gaunt and gray-haired with a kindly expression on his face. He wore no hat, but a white muffler was wrapped closely about his neck. The muffler was very white and his overcoat was very black and he had the queerest blue eyes. In the light that shone through the door Judy could see him distinctly and yet, for the barest moment, she had thought there was nobody there.

Then he spoke and Judy was startled at the quiet tone of his voice.

"May I inquire who lives here?"

For a moment Judy could only stare at him. What a strange question! The doctor's sign was displayed in prominent letters on the window and right underneath was a plate that also said, H. H. BOLTON, M.D. He must have seen it when she turned on the light.

"Dr. Bolton lives here," she replied. "I'm his daughter, Judy Bolton."

She expected his slow smile, but not the strange look he gave her. Judy's midnight visitor was looking, not at her, but right through her to something else beyond. He didn't seem to see her at all.

She shivered, half-closing the door against the wind. It blew his coat tails and his white muffler. But, unmindful of it, he went on speaking in the same quiet tone.

"I just wanted to know," he said. "Is there anyone else?"

"Just my family. There are others in the house now, of course, because we're having a party."

"The others are quiet," he said, turning his head.

"They're hiding," Judy told him. "You see, you interrupted a game. They're keeping quiet because they don't want anybody to find them."

"I think I'd enjoy playing games in this house again," the stranger said. His voice had a sad quality that Judy had not noticed before. It seemed to hold the memory of long-ago, beautiful things. Something Sally had said flashed across her mind—'Everything is probably very beautiful to ghosts.'

"Who are you?" she demanded suddenly. "Why have you come here and how can you stand there talking so calmly in such a storm?"

"I don't mind the storm," he replied. "I just stopped by for a visit because I used to live here. I was fond of the place. It was the only real home I ever had. I climbed this tree above our heads and my brothers and I raced through those halls and down those stairs." He waved a thin hand in the general direction of the house. "I only wanted to find out if any of the Vincents live here now."

"They never did—so far as I know," Judy added, realizing how little she knew about the history of the house. "Harry Vincent owned it once, but he rented it. I don't think he ever lived here."

"But the Vincent girl came to your party——"

"I know," Judy replied, "but she went away again."

"Could you tell me where?"

"I'm afraid I couldn't." He seemed to be moving away from her as she talked. "Are you a relative?"

"Her uncle, but I think she's afraid of me——"

"Not her uncle Ned!" Judy exclaimed, taking a step toward him and then finding herself pushed back again by the wind. "Wait a minute! We've been wanting to see you——"

But he had turned and was beginning to go down the steps, his cane tap-tapping as he walked. The wind grew stronger.

"Wait a minute!" Judy cried again. "You can't go out in this storm. It isn't safe. Can't you see how the branches are cracking off the trees? It isn't safe to walk under them. Please come back! I wanted to see you. If I had known who you were I would have asked you in before!"

She was beckoning frantically, but the stranger paid no attention. He continued walking, as though he neither saw nor heard her, his cane tapping and his white muffler waving like a flag.

"It isn't safe!" she called still louder.

But when she attempted to follow him she was almost blown off the steps.

"Wait! Wait!" she shrieked above the wind.

The others had abandoned their game and rushed to the door, her mother with them. Dr. Bolton was not there. He had been called to the hospital earlier in the evening and expected to be there all night.

"Who was it?" several voices asked.

"I—I—" Judy clutched at the porch post; just saved herself from falling. An enormous crash sounded all around her, shaking the whole house and the grounds around it.

Crack! Splinter! Crash! And the tree was down. The big hollow tree that had stood like a landmark in front of Judy's house now lay directly across the walk, its branches extending the full length of the lawn and blocking the garage driveway. The wind had overturned it, roots and all, and it had fallen between Judy and the man she had been trying to call in out of the storm.

She covered her face with her hands to shut out the sight; then realized, more sensibly, that the tree couldn't have hit him. He had just about reached the gate when it fell. Whether he had turned up or down Grove Street she could not say. He was gone and all the answer she had for their many questions was that a man had called for Kay Vincent and she believed it must have been her uncle Ned.

"But Judy, he's the one we wanted to see!" cried Peter, growing excited. "Why didn't you tell him we wanted to see him? Why didn't you call him in?"

"I did! Couldn't you hear me calling? Of course I called, but he just kept on walking and then the tree fell and I couldn't see him any more."

"Of course you couldn't," said Marge, looking skeptical. "How could you see Ned Vincent when he's dead?"

Judy stared at her a moment and then all the color drained out of her face.

"He died only a month ago," Marge continued relentlessly. "Betty and I were at the funeral. I guess we ought to know that he couldn't come back."

"But he said he was her uncle," Judy insisted tonelessly.

"Well, he couldn't have been. Both her uncles are dead. If there was anybody there, which I very much doubt, it was some crook posing as her uncle——"

"Or a ghost," put in the more credulous Betty. "I always did believe this house was haunted."

"So did I," echoed some of the others.

"Sometimes, on a night like this," Scottie spoke up, "the atmosphere does form strange images. It might have formed the image of someone who had once stood there and—and didn't any more."

"That's a scientific fact," Horace added, supporting her statement. "Only recently I read an article about damp weather ghosts. It's something like the mirages people see in the desert. Well, couldn't this man Judy thought she saw have been a sort of mirage?"

They kept on talking like that and soon Judy was asking herself, had he really been there.

"Did you see him, Honey? Did you, Mother? Did you? Did you?"

They all answered in the negative. Not one of them had seen the curious figure in the black coat and the white muffler. Not one of them had heard the tapping sound that Judy described. Peter put his arm around her and pulled her into the living room.

"We've all had too big a day, Judy girl. We're all unstrung," he said. "Your midnight visitor was probably some branch that blew against the bell and made it ring."

"No, Peter, no! He spoke to me," Judy declared. "He said he used to live here. Used to! Just as if he didn't live anywhere any more. And he looked—remember how Sally said her ghost looked, just as though he didn't see you at all, but saw something else?"

"Judy, you're imagining——"

"I don't. You know that."

They were all crowding around her—her mother, the Hamilton girls, Selma, Scottie . . .

"Maybe he's what Sally saw," Tag suggested. "She ran to the window and saw something and then she and I hid under the table. She's still there, I guess."

"Let's ask her," Honey said.

They tiptoed into the dining room. Just why they went on tiptoe none of them could have said, unless it was to surprise Sally under the table. She was still there, huddled in a forlorn little heap. She looked out at Judy, her eyes dark with fright.

"Is he—is he gone?"

"Is who gone?" asked Judy sharply.

"Your midnight visitor," wailed Sally. "I saw him! I knew he'd follow me here. It isn't the house that's haunted, Judy, it's me-ee!"

"You're not being very brave," Horace reminded her.

"She's hysterical—" Marge began.

"I am not hysterical!" cried Sally, bumping her head on the underneath part of the table as she scrambled out.

"Come now," Horace said more gently, "tell us about it. What did you see?"

"The gho-ost!" quavered Sally. "He's the same ghost I saw outside that other house— when I hid—under the she-ets."

"Well, he's gone now," Peter told her reassuringly. "Come on, let's get on with our game. I can't take you girls home in the car now. I can't use the car myself until that fallen tree's been chopped up and taken away."

"I always liked that tree," sighed Horace.

"You would!" Peter returned with an attempt at joking to cheer everybody up and make Judy forget the apparition. "If I remember correctly, it was in that hollow tree that you found a quantity of Vine Thompson's stolen jewels. It was one of the biggest scoops the newspaper ever had."

"But that wasn't all." Horace refused to be cheered. "The tree was part of this place. It sort of belonged here——"

"I feel that way about it too," Judy said.

"Well, there's no use crying over spilt milk or fallen trees either," Betty Hamilton spoke up unsympathetically. "Are we going ahead with the game or aren't we?"

"I don't want to play any more," Judy told her. "Our midnight visitor has made it all a little too exciting. Suppose he should come again!"

"He won't. He probably wasn't there in the first place," Scottie said.

"And it was my turn to be detective," Marge protested. "I haven't had a turn."

"That's right," Honey agreed. "Marge deserves a turn the same as the rest of us. Please, Judy, let's play just this one more time."

"Please!" coaxed Selma in her plaintive, persuasive voice. "Tag and I were having such a good time and you know what fun we always have when we play Murder at our house."

"Your house is different——" Judy began.

"If it's on account of me," Sally put in, "you don't need to worry. I'm always getting scared of things. The—the family tell me I'm slightly queer. Maybe I fell on my head or something."

"Oh, Sally! You didn't either," laughed Tag. "We all like you."

"Then don't let me spoil your fun."

"It isn't that," Judy said. "It's just that it's so late and we're all tired and our nerves are on edge. There's a lot to do tomorrow too. We're going down to the courthouse and you're going to tell me about that mysterious family. I know this party can't break up until the wind quiets down, but if we must play games, can't we play something a little more quiet?"

"Truth and consequences," suggested Horace from the corner over by the parrot's cage.

"You cheat!" squawked the parrot from under his cover.

"Now if we could murder that parrot," said Judy, "there might be some point in the game. But, since we can't, I still think that something a little more quiet might be more suitable."

"Murder's quiet," Selma insisted, "especially when we're hiding. We have to be quiet or we can't hear the victim scream."

Judy gave it up.

"Very well, if you must play Murder, you couldn't have found a more appropriate time and place."

CHAPTER X

A DISAPPEARANCE

Judy's objections ruled out, Horace began passing the cards for another game of Murder. First he took one himself and then held out the pack to Judy. She looked at her card and then turned it over quickly. She was "it" this time, but no one must know it. That was for the detective to find out when the lights were snapped on again after the game.

When the cards had all been passed, glanced at and collected again, somebody turned out the lights. Judy backed up against the archway between the living room and the dining room, waiting for someone to pass.

As she waited in the darkness, she heard hurrying feet, banging doors and the usual low whistles and cat calls.

"This suspense is terrible," a voice whispered quite close to her. She heard footsteps coming nearer, more whispered voices and all at once a piercing scream rang out.

95

"Somebody's been murdered!" a chorus of voices called.

Lights were snapped on as Marge, the detective, came up from the cellar where she had been waiting. Blackberry followed. The cat had been following people up and down the cellar stairs all evening, enjoying the excitement, but now his tail bristled.

"Where is the victim?" Marge asked, assuming the air of a professional sleuth. "I heard somebody scream. Stay where you are, everybody! Where is the victim?"

Usually the person who had been murdered immediately stretched himself out and pretended to be dead. With much laughing and joking, flowers were placed in his hand and then, while the corpse giggled occasionally, the trial proceeded. But this time nobody was stretched out on the floor or the sofa or anywhere.

"Who screamed?" everybody began asking everybody else.

Horace and Peter admitted to the whistles and cat calls. Selma said she and Tag were whispering and pretending to moan. But they hadn't screamed.

"Betty was whispering too," Tag added. "I guess we all were."

"I wasn't," declared Scottie. "I was hiding alone."

"Were you whispering, Honey?" asked Marge.

She shook her head. "I was hiding behind the parrot's cage. I didn't dare."

"Maybe the parrot screamed."

"He squawks," said Horace. "No, for once, the parrot is innocent."

"Anyway," Honey added, "if he had screamed I would have known it. I was within six inches of his cage."

"It must have been Sally then," Marge said at last. "Everybody else is here."

Judy still stood in the doorway wondering what to do. This was a queer turn of affairs. She was "it" and she hadn't found her victim. Nobody was supposed to scream until she was ready.

"But I was the murderer," she said, revealing the secret that the detective was supposed to discover at the mock trial. "I hadn't begun to play——"

"Then somebody else tried to horn in," Horace declared. "That isn't fair. It spoils the whole game if everybody goes around making believe to be 'it.' "

"Maybe nobody did. It isn't a murder any-way," laughed Scottie, still in the spirit of the game. "It's just a disappearance. Where's Sally?"

"Sally! Sally!" they all began calling. "Come out! The game's over. We're ready to have the trial."

"She must be hiding outside," Tag spoke up. "She brushed past me in the dark. She and another girl were going in the direction of the front door."

"She wouldn't try to hide on the porch, would she—in this storm?"

They looked and were glad to be inside again away from the wind.

"It all boils down to a single question then," Marge announced, still playing detec-tive. "Who was the girl Tag saw with Sally?"

"The murderer, of course," laughed Honey. "She concealed her victim."

"But I was the murderer," Judy insisted. "I drew the card. I stood there in the doorway waiting until someone should pass. I tell you, I wasn't ready yet. It wasn't fair for anybody else to scream——"

"Sometimes people scream when they aren't playing a game," Peter announced grimly. "I propose we forget all this nonsense and start a serious search for Sally. If she's anywhere in the house we're bound to find her."

"She must be in the house unless—" Judy stopped short, suddenly realizing the seriousness of the situation. "Tag, are you quite sure she and the other girl were on their way toward the front door?"

She nodded. "But I couldn't see the other girl. I only recognized Sally because she brushed past me and that blue silk rustles. You know how dark it is with the lights out."

Judy knew. But this was alarming.

"Tag," she demanded, "if you couldn't see, then how could you know it was another girl. Couldn't it have been—a boy, maybe—or a man?"

Hearing their alarmed voices, Mrs. Bolton hurried downstairs again and wanted to know what was wrong.

"It's Sally!" Judy cried. "We were just playing but when the lights went on again we couldn't find her."

Mrs. Bolton didn't say, as any mother might have been tempted to do, that she never had approved of playing games in the dark. There wasn't time for that. Instead, she sensibly joined in organizing the searching party that Peter had suggested. Horace was determined to go out into the storm.

"It's what any decent fellow would do," he declared. "Mother, you and the girls can search inside the house. Peter and I will go outside and find out just what happened when that tree fell across the walk."

"But Horace," they all protested, "the tree fell before Sally disappeared, not afterwards."

Horace was not to be moved by any argument.

"Just the same, it must have had something to do with it. Sally might have tried to hide under it. Those upturned roots may have formed some sort of a trap."

"The tunnel down cellar is the only trap I can think of!" Judy exclaimed as she grabbed Honey's hand and dashed for the stairs. Blackberry squirmed in ahead of them and they almost tripped over him in their haste.

"Sally!" Judy called. "Sally! Sally! Are you down here?"

The hollow echo of her voice was her only answer.

She threw open the trap door in the floor of the cellar while Honey held the light and flashed it into the opening.

"Sally! Sally!" she called again.

Her echo answered from the tunnel, almost like a human voice. But there was no other sound.

"It doesn't seem likely she'd be down here," Judy decided after one glance inside the second cellar. "It's dark and wet and she seemed so proud of her new clothes. But if she had gone into the tunnel——"

Honey shuddered.

"Didn't you say the tunnel was flooded?"

"Yes, but Sally can swim. I wonder how deep the water is. It might be dangerous trying to swim through from this end. I'm going to test it," Judy announced, pulling off her dress and shoes almost in the same instant.

"Wish me luck!" she called, trying to be cheerful as she began descending.

At the foot of the ladder she stepped into the muddy second cellar. The water seemed to have gone down a little but it was still up to her ankles and then to her knees as she walked farther toward the tunnel. Just where she knew it dipped, she paused a minute, shivering at the thought of diving in.

"But if Sally could swim through it," she told herself, "so can I."

Honey was still holding the light, sending its beam clear across the flooded tunnel.

"Here goes!" called Judy in a brave voice as she let herself down.

The water was thick with slime. She swam in it only a moment and then discovered that, when she stood up in the deepest part of the pool, the water came to her chin. As she searched, she kept calling back reassuring words to Honey.

"It isn't cold!" And to herself, "It's like ice!"

"Is there anything in it?" Honey called out.

Anything? Judy shuddered. That was just it. There might be anything. Then she remembered something and called back cheerfully, "There's a drain somewhere if I can find it . . . Oh, here it is!" She stubbed her toe against the round piece of tile through which water was supposed to flow out of the tunnel. It smarted a little but she didn't stop to find out whether or not it was badly bruised. "The drain must be clogged. I think I'll dive in and pull away whatever's stopping it——"

"Judy! Don't!" protested Honey.

Then she heard a gurgle as Judy went under and waited, holding the light and almost holding her breath until she should come up again.

There was another gurgle and the sound of water draining out.

"I've done it!" Judy announced presently. "It was just a lot of papers—some of those old Vine used to wrap around her wine bottles, I guess. They smell of it and heaven only knows what else. But anyway, you can hear the water."

"I hear it all right. I thought for a minute you weren't coming up."

"If I intended to drown myself," said Judy with a laugh that promptly turned to a shiver, "I'd choose *clean* water. It's freezing down here. Honey, please hand me that old sweater of Horace's. See it? There on the hook just behind the work-bench. The cellar will be dry in a minute," she added as she shrugged into the sweater, "and we can start looking for clues."

"Do you see any tracks down there?" Honey inquired, bending farther over with the light. "You ought to be able to see them in that soft mud."

In the excitement, Judy had not thought of looking for tracks. Now her own footprints could be seen distinctly. Sally's were there too. It was easy to tell they were Sally's because of the small shoe the girl wore. But the footprints went mostly in one direction. Sally might easily have made them when she swam in through the tunnel and, from there, entered the secret cellar where she claimed she had found the empty tin box.

"Honey!" Judy shouted. "Is there a box up there on the work-bench? Sally found one and put it there—an empty tin box."

There was a pause while Honey looked around and Judy continued to examine the footprints that criss-crossed the muddy second cellar.

"I don't see any box," she answered at last. "How big was it?"

"Oh, about as big as a shoe box. It was tin, painted black and a little rusty at the edges."

"There's no such box here."

"Are you sure?" asked Judy in surprise.

When Honey answered that she was quite sure, Judy climbed up the ladder to see for herself. She was muddy and chilled, but more than anything else, she was completely mystified. Could Sally have taken the box with her and, if so, had it really been empty? Even if it had, where could she have found it and why had she attempted to conceal it behind her back? There was certainly something strange about a box that had suddenly appeared out of nowhere, just as the girl had, and then vanished in the same mysterious manner. Either Sally had taken the box and gone away of her own free will—*but where?* Or else somebody had taken both Sally and the box and that scream Judy had heard was Sally's call for help.

"Maybe somebody she knew found out she was here and took her home," Honey suggested. "She mentioned a family and she would have screamed if she had tried to run away from them and then been taken back home against her will—wherever her home is," she added in bewilderment as she took Judy's arm. "Let's go back to the living room. Maybe Peter and Horace have found out something—or the girls who are searching upstairs."

CHAPTER XI

A HALF hour later they were all in the living room again. The searching party that had been organized had combed the entire house and grounds. Scottie had courageously searched the attic and found nothing but dust and cob-webs. Nobody had been up there for some time, she felt quite certain.

Betty and Marge had looked in the upstairs rooms.

"We had an idea that Sally had simply grown tired of the game and fallen asleep on some-body's bed," Marge explained, "but she wasn't on them or under them or in any of the closets."

Selma and Tag had hunted through the down-stairs rooms, peeking into all the hiding places. While they made almost a game of it, Mrs. Bolton had crossed the hall and searched the doctor's office and reception room.

"Even though they were locked," she ex-plained, "I thought it was a wise precaution. Sally might have had the key."

106

Horace and Peter were drenched to the skin and huddled around the fireplace warming themselves. They had succeeded in chopping a few branches off the tree, enough so that now they were quite sure nothing could be pinned under it. Horace was obliged to abandon his idea of a trap. The tree had blocked the walk and the garage driveway and that was all. When they had time they would chop it up and store the pieces for firewood. All winter the Boltons would be burning pieces of the tree that used to shade the porch and sometimes tap with its branches against the windows. After the tree was removed, Peter could get his car out of the garage, but not until then. Horace, who had taken it upon himself to search the garage as well, reported that everything was just as Peter had left it. He stood running his fingers through his hair and thinking.

"It's too bad we didn't get that kid's story out of her tonight," he said. "It's just possible she ran away because she didn't want us to hear it."

"But Horace," his mother protested, "a child like that could have nothing very terrible to conceal. It may have been something that frightened her and made her run away."

"Judy! That man you saw!" Scottie exclaimed. "Sally said he'd follow her here."

"Maybe it was Ned Vincent," Betty spoke up. "Lots of people believe in ghosts and they're said to haunt the houses where they used to live. Didn't he look the least bit strange?"

"It was only his eyes and that vague way he had," Judy answered. "I can see why Sally would be frightened but I can't believe he would have come back and spirited her away."

"I was right about the midnight visitor," Peter remarked, "though I only said it in fun. But it's true, Judy, you never have gone into the history of this house. Does anybody know? Did the Vincents really used to live here?"

Marge thought that they had. The Hamiltons were old friends of the Vincents.

"Mother often spoke of the Vincent boys. There were just the three of them," she said. "Harry was the oldest; Lou was next and Ned was six or seven years younger. They went into business together but there was some quarrel over furniture polish at the time Lou was burned. Ned, the younger brother, sold out his interest in the furniture factory and bought that house below Roulsville where the Vincents are living now."

"That was Ned's house then? Not Lou's?" Peter questioned.

"But he bought it only seven years ago," Marge put in before he had time to question her further. "They must have lived in this house years ago. Harry Vincent could have purchased it from his father's estate or his father could have sold it and then Harry could have bought it back again."

"That's possible," Judy agreed, trying to connect things in her own mind. As she remembered the story, he had bought it intending to rent it to the new foreman at the furniture factory but had charged so much rent that the foreman had refused his offer. Shortly after that Vine Thompson had moved in to begin her business of buying and selling stolen goods. It was about this same time that Harry Vincent had remodeled the house and had, Judy felt sure, either built or enlarged the second cellar and the secret tunnel. Stolen goods were smuggled through from cars housed innocently in the garage.

That, so far as she knew, was the story up until the time of Vine Thompson's murder. After that the haunted house rumor had started and a number of families had moved in and out again in rapid succession, being frightened away by so-called ghosts. Judy thought she had explained them all. She had certainly tried. But here the house was, as Horace put it, just as haunted as ever. They might talk over its history until morning without finding a trace of Sally.

The strange part of it, to Judy's mind, was that now they had found another haunted house —haunted, so Sally claimed, by the same ghost. The two houses were enough alike to be twins. But had the other house been remodeled with a second cellar and a tunnel too? That might explain the mysterious light. It might explain a lot of things, especially if the owner happened to be Harry Vincent.

"I don't like the similarity between this house and the other one," Judy said thoughtfully. "Let's take a trip over there tomorrow and have a look around."

Betty looked horrified.

"Judy, would you *dare?*"

"I dared dive into that pool down cellar, didn't I?" she answered. "Besides, even if the place is haunted, Sally said the ghosts never try to hurt anybody."

"But Ned Vincent is dead."

"That makes him even less dangerous," Judy declared. "He appeared to me to be a very gentle spirit—not at all as I had imagined Kay's uncle. You know, Harry Vincent claims he forged his brother Lou's will."

"Rather a shame, I think," remarked Horace, "to drag his name into court when he's dead and can't defend himself."

"If I had known that—" began Peter, and then he closed his lips tightly as though he had decided not to say whatever he had been thinking.

"I should have asked him sooner," lamented Judy. "He would have been willing to talk with us, I'm sure. He said this house was the only real home he ever had. And he seemed so sad about it, just as though he never expected to have another. He mentioned playing games and running through the halls and up the stairs and climbing that tree—and now it isn't there any more."

She finished her sentence with a little catch in her voice and Mrs. Bolton put an arm gently around her.

"Perhaps it was only Dr. Burlingame and he had the houses confused. People say he's grown a little eccentric. There was some tragedy. But your father can tell you all about it in the morning. You're tired now. You must let your friends go home and get a little rest yourself. I really think the police ought to be told about Sally. But Peter will see to that."

"What about me?" demanded Horace. "You don't think I'm going to wait around for things to happen, do you? The newspaper can help as well as the police. Don't worry, Mom, if I'm not back until morning."

"Don't forget to tell them where we found Sally!" Judy called just as he hurried out of the door.

Marge turned to her. "How can he tell them anything when he doesn't even know her name?"

"Wasn't it Burlingame?" questioned Scottie with a yawn. "You introduced her as Sally Burlingame."

"The name was entirely my idea," Judy confessed. "It was on the mail box in front of the other house."

"Couldn't Sally have lived there?"

"I don't think so." Judy paused, stroking Blackberry. The cat always came to comfort her whenever her voice sounded troubled. "No, I think she went there to look for something— and she was looking for something here."

"Maybe she went away because she found it."

Betty rose to her feet with dignity. "Wherever she went," she announced, "I'm going home. Peter can't take us in his car but we can still call a taxi. We can carry Tag if necessary." She began shaking her younger sister while Marge made the call. Tag and Selma had both fallen asleep on the sofa. "Wake up, Tag!" she ordered roughly. "We're going home now. It isn't polite to fall asleep on other people's furniture."

Tag opened her eyes. "Is it morning?" she inquired drowsily.

"No, but it soon will be. Wake up! There's a taxi coming."

This roused her. Tag seldom had a chance to ride in taxis. The Hamilton girls invited Honey to ride with them but Mrs. Bolton persuaded Peter to stay until the doctor came home.

"We may need you," she said, "as nobody seems to know what will happen in this house next."

"Good night, Judy!" called Scottie as Selma stumbled along after her. The wind had quieted down now and they had only to run next door.

"We'll be waiting to hear what happens," Honey said as she pulled on her raincoat.

The taxi horn sounded outside the house.

"Good night, Judy!" Marge called from the door. Her little sister changed it to "Good morning!" for it was after three o'clock.

"Goodbye, Judy," said Betty. "Thanks for a thrilling party. Oh, I almost forgot to tell you. We were all so excited over that ghost you saw. But just before Sally disappeared Kay Vincent called and drove right away again. She has her own car, you know. She seemed to be in sort of a hurry."

CHAPTER XII

JUDY was absolutely stunned for a moment. She glared at the panels of the closed front door and then turned to Peter.

"Now why couldn't Betty have told me that before?" she demanded. "If Sally was frightened and Kay had a car the first thing that would have entered her head, I should think, would have been that Kay took Sally with her."

"But Kay wouldn't pick up a stranger," Peter said. "Kay's not that kind."

"Maybe she wasn't a stranger. Maybe she knew Kay. Peter, did you ever stop to think that perhaps Sally was one of Kay's relatives? Would that mean anything to you? Would that explain anything? Why, the minute we mentioned Kay Vincent's name she stiffened a little and then got curious. Can you see why? Her name must be Vincent too and she only kept quiet because she realized I hated the whole Vincent tribe and she wanted me to like her. Sally Vincent! That must be her name. And

115

the girl Tag saw her with was probably Kay. She called for her and left quietly and that solves the whole mystery.''

Peter looked thoughtful for a moment. Then he said, ''I suppose that accounts for her being alone in Dr. Burlingame's house and thinking she saw a ghost and——''

''Wait a minute!'' exclaimed Judy, holding up her hand. ''I guess I'm too anxious. It doesn't solve so very much after all, does it? It doesn't begin to explain why she was hunting around in the cellar or what she expected to find. What would there be left for the Vincents to find in our house?''

''Didn't you mention a box that disappeared?''

''Yes, but Sally claimed it was empty.''

''Perhaps its contents are still in the house then. It's just possible they may have had something to do with Lou Vincent's will.''

''Do you really think so?'' Judy cried excitedly. ''Oh, Peter! This is going to be a real mystery case. I just can't wait until tomorrow morning when we go down to the courthouse.''

''There won't be very much time to wait,'' her mother put in, ''unless you begin thinking about getting some rest.''

"But how can I rest, Mother, when we don't know where Sally is?"

"You can easily find out if she went home with Kay. The Vincents have a telephone, don't they? Why not call them up?"

"Of course," agreed Judy. "Mother, you angel to think of it. If I know Sally's safe I can go to bed and sleep like a top for what's left of the night."

Although it was an unearthly hour for anybody's telephone to ring, Judy made the call. After the bell had buzzed for several minutes Harry Vincent's voice answered. It was decidedly gruff and unpleasant.

"No, of course Kay isn't here," he replied to Judy's question. "She expected to spend the night with friends in Farringdon. And as for any relatives she may have, if you and Peter Dobbs had been interested I would have told you. But apparently he thinks more of those high-sounding speeches he heard in law school than he does of an actual case. You can tell him, Miss Judy Bolton, that Mr. Sanders and I won't require his services."

"But Mr. Vincent——"

"I've no more to say. I suppose you know it's nearly morning."

With that he hung up and Judy turned tragic eyes to Peter. In a flash she realized all that this case must have meant to him. It would have given him the best possible legal experience. With a real mystery angle to it, he would have learned more from it than from a dozen ordinary cases. Handwriting experts, doctors, employees, witnesses to the will, as well as friends and relatives would be called in to testify and, while Peter would not have questioned them himself, he would have been able to suggest questions for Mr. Sanders to ask. He would have helped prepare the case and, even if Harry Vincent's side had lost it, there would still have been money in it. With two aged grandparents to support, Judy knew that Peter had need of all the money he could honestly earn. He had a housekeeper for his grandmother now and his grandfather was far too feeble to engage in any active work. Honey expected to secure a position as a designer of fashions in Brandt's Department store but, so far, she was only on the waiting list of applicants. There were so many people depending on Peter—his grandparents, his sister, even Judy herself. And she had wanted so much to help!

"I've spoiled your case," she burst out at last, facing him. "Harry Vincent doesn't want you any more and it's all my fault. Oh, Peter! I'm too dumb to be anybody's secretary. I should have taken Dad's advice and gone to c-college."

She was sobbing now, in gulps like a very little girl. Peter made a few gestures but he never knew what to do with girls who cried. Her mother handed her a handkerchief.

"Come dear," she said, "it isn't as bad as that. There will be other cases."

"If you're worrying about me," Peter told her huskily, "forget it. I'll get on somehow with the little business. As a matter of fact, I had just about decided not to monkey with this case anyway. Horace is right. It is a shame to drag Ned Vincent's name into court when he's dead and can't defend himself. I intended to tell Harry Vincent——"

"That's just it!" Judy interrupted tearfully. "You intended to tell him. But now he's told you and that makes all the difference."

Peter was silent. It did make some difference. He couldn't deny that.

Very little was said about it when Dr. Bolton came in five minutes later. The doctor was

tired. He had just finished an emergency operation and had not expected to find his family still
up when he came home.

"Whatever's troubling you, Judy girl," he
said, "it isn't as important right now as getting
some sleep. You know I don't believe in young
girls keeping such late hours. Don't you see
enough of Peter all day at the office?"

"But Dad," she protested. "Something terrible has happened——"

"It may not be as terrible as you think,"
Peter interrupted, suddenly cheerful as he took
his hat and prepared to go. "I've just been
thinking that Sally may have something to do
with this will. She didn't ask all those questions
about it for nothing. Judy, I still intend to look
it over in the morning and if you want to go
with me, you'll have to take your father's advice and get some sleep. Now that we know
Ned Vincent is dead, I'm curious to see just
who does get Lou's property."

"Maybe it's Sally!" Judy exclaimed, wide-
eyed; forgetting her tears. "Maybe the Vincent girl the—the ghost spoke of was Sally . . .
not Kay. Oh, Peter! Maybe they're trying to
hurt her."

"I rather think," Peter agreed, "that she

may be the person they're fighting. If she is then I certainly would have refused to assist in the case. It would have been a satisfaction," he added, "to have been able to refuse."

The wind was dying down and, when Peter had left, an unnatural stillness settled over the house. Judy knew she should be tired but still she lingered a moment, trying to think. Sally had wanted to go down to the courthouse with them but for some other reason, she had said, than merely to look at the will.

"Don't try to puzzle out anything more to-night, Judy girl," her mother told her, appearing at the door with a glass of hot lemonade in her hands. "Drink this, and here's a white tablet to go with it. It's your father's orders. It will quiet your nerves and keep you from catching cold unless," she added, "you've already waited too long after that chilling you had."

Judy took it dutifully and went to her room, but not to sleep. Everywhere about her were things to remind her of Sally—the tracks on the stairs, the towel she had used and then thrown carelessly over the chair, the pink and white blanket she had wrapped around her. In the bath room her muddy clothes were probably

still in the hamper. But were they? Suddenly
curious, Judy hurried in to see.

She lifted the cover. Her own clothes were on
top just as she had left them and, underneath,
Sally's. Why, that was the first thing a real
detective would do—search the clothes for laun-
dry marks, initials and, naturally, hunt through
the pockets.

Sally's underthings revealed nothing except
the trade mark, PRINCESS. Princess slips
and underwear were sold everywhere. But the
dress had a pocket and in the pocket was a
folded piece of water-soaked paper and a handkerchief with the initial V.

"Vincent," Judy murmured, "just as I
thought. She must be Ned Vincent's little girl.
And her mother is dead too. Poor Sally!"

Piece by piece, Judy unfolded the paper, being careful not to tear it. She had carried the
things back into her own room and now spread
the damp, torn paper on her bed. Very dim
pencil marks were on it and at first she could
not make them out. They looked like figures.
She held her magnifying glass over the paper.
Yes, they were figures:

$$7 \times 7$$

—and that was all. What could it mean?
Perhaps nothing more than the fact that Sally
had been trying to learn her multiplication
tables. Judy guessed her age as about fourteen and certainly she ought to know them if she
had attended school at all regularly.

Seven times seven?

Well, it could stand for forty-nine of something. Or it could locate something—seven
steps one way and seven steps another. Seven
checks one way on the blanket and seven checks
the other. What nonsense! Judy knew now
that she must have some sleep or she wouldn't
be able even to think properly.

The mysterious paper she placed carefully
inside the secret drawer in her dresser that she
kept for clues. Then, exhausted, she pulled on
her pajamas and crawled into bed, still thinking
of things that might be counted by sevens.

CHAPTER XIII

When Judy awoke the next morning her head ached and her throat felt as though a piece of sandpaper had been rubbed over it.

"Dad's right," she thought, "a young girl shouldn't keep such late hours."

The happenings of the previous night now seemed more impossible than ever. Perhaps she had been a little delirious and talked to something that wasn't there when she thought she saw that man with the black coat and the white muffler and the queer eyes that didn't seem to look at her, but at something else.

Horace came in, surprised that Judy should still be in bed, and thrust the *Daily Herald* before her face. He had succeeded in getting his story in just before the paper went to press. It was in prominent type on the lower section of the front page. With the unbounded faith of a young reporter, he believed a front page story was all-important.

"Newspaper stories," he declared, "solve more mysteries than detective agencies ever do. Look at this, Sis. Shouldn't it get a rise out of somebody?"

Judy opened the paper and read:

GIRL SEES GHOST
ATTENDS PARTY AND IS MYSTERI- OUSLY SPIRITED AWAY

Farringdon, June 24th. A girl who called herself Sally and refused to give any other name was discovered hiding in an apparently empty house by Peter Dobbs, Roulsville's up-and-coming young lawyer and our local girl detective, Judy Bolton.

Judy looked up. "I don't like that title," she said, a little hoarsely for her throat hurt like anything. "Couldn't you have thought of something more original?"

"Don't pick it to pieces," Horace scolded her. "Go on! Read it."

"I'm reading it," she said. "Horace, this is going to make somebody mad enough to tear himself in two and, if a hunch Peter and I have is right, that somebody is Harry Vincent."

"I guess I haven't heard the whole story then. I intended to add to it when we call on

Dr. Burlingame. I rather suspect him of being your midnight visitor. But what is it you've found out?''

"Nothing definite," she admitted. "But if Ned Vincent is dead then somebody else must get that property his brother willed to him. Now, it's just possible that somebody may be Sally. I don't suppose you'd know whether or not either of the Vincent brothers had a daughter.''

"I know Lou didn't," Horace told her. "I never heard a thing about Ned."

"Well, if Sally should be Ned's daughter, then she's the one the Vincents are trying to cheat out of her property. She isn't a princess in disguise but she may easily be a little heiress. You know, wills usually say 'his heirs and assigns forever.' I'll have to ask Peter who his assigns would be. For all I'm a lawyer's secretary, I'm awfully dumb about law."

"You figured that out and still dare call yourself dumb?"

"I just happened to find a handkerchief with an initial V on it in Sally's pocket. There was a paper too, but it didn't seem to have much meaning. Peter helped put the puzzle together. We talked till four o'clock. I guess that's why

I'm so hoarse this morning. Dad finally ordered me to bed with some sort of medicine that made me sleep. What time is it, Horace?"

"Exactly eleven thirty," he told her, turning her little clock around so that she could see it. "No wonder you couldn't tell with poor Tick Tock's face to the wall. I suppose you're getting up for lunch?"

"If I don't," Judy said, "Dad will probably take my temperature and discover I have a fever. I've been trying to tell myself I was delirious last night but, no matter how I figure it, I still recall it all as something that really happened. You should have headed your news item·

JUDY BOLTON SEES GHOST
INSISTS THAT DEAD MAN CALLED
AT HER DOOR."

"That would make a story," Horace agreed. "But it might put you in a bad light, Judy. I don't want people telling me my sister is slightly unbalanced——"

"Horace Bolton! Take that back!" cried Judy, throwing her pillow. He ducked it and it just missed the light. "Now stay out until

I'm dressed. If Mother should ask you, tell her I'm feeling fine. I expect to be allowed to go down to the court house with Peter when he calls.''

''He telephoned about an hour ago and said he'd be here at one o'clock,'' Horace said and then went noisily down the stairs.

Judy glanced again at her clock. That didn't give her much time if she expected to have lunch with the family. She dressed hurriedly in a navy blue suit that made her look a little older than she was. Then, because her throat still felt sore, she gargled it several times with soda and water just before going downstairs.

The Boltons usually had lunch promptly at noon. The doctor's office hours were from one until three and again in the evening from seven until eight. Judy was anxious to see him. She seated herself at the table and unfolded her napkin.

''I suppose Mother has already told you about the excitement last night,'' she said, taking a spoonful of soup and discovering that it hurt her to swallow.

''She told me a great deal,'' he replied slowly. ''I must confess, it left me bewildered. I'm waiting to hear more from you.''

"There's nothing more, I guess, except that I found Sally's handkerchief with an initial V on it. That makes me more certain than ever that she's some relative of Kay's."

"A cousin, perhaps," her mother put in.

"Well, whatever she was, Harry Vincent wouldn't admit it," Judy declared. "Horace, did you hear that he practically kicked Peter out of the case? It seemed to me that the sky was falling then, but afterwards Peter said he wouldn't have helped at the trial anyway if they're trying to cheat Sally."

Dr. Bolton tasted his coffee and then put the cup down thoughtfully.

"It's odd that you should have met her in Dr. Burlingame's house," he said. "You know that he was an old friend of mine?"

"Mother told me. Tell me about him, Dad."

"Well," her father began, "he was once a prominent doctor here in Farringdon. He specialized in eye, ear, nose and throat troubles."

Judy gulped, hoping her father wouldn't notice that she was having a little throat trouble herself. Eating the soup was an effort although, as a rule, she was especially fond of her mother's home-made chicken gumbo.

"I was practicing in Roulsville when I first met Dr. Burlingame," her father went on. "A great many of the families we know now used to call him in for special cases. Sometimes he would be called to Roulsville. I called him several times myself when a consultation of doctors seemed necessary. To call in Dr. Burlingame, in those days, meant that a patient would be given a specialist's care. But about five years ago there was some tragedy in his family and he gave up practicing. His daughter ran away and then his wife died very suddenly. I only saw the doctor once after that. He seemed to have aged twenty years."

"You wouldn't know whether or not he still lives in that house on the road that turns off just above Roulsville, would you? There was a telephone there but the phone book lists no such name."

"Perhaps it's a private wire," he answered. "I've heard that the doctor became a recluse after his wife died, closed up his house and, when he was there, refused to see visitors. I believe, for a time, he was confined in an institution."

"It's true then!" Judy exclaimed. "Marge Hamilton said he was a little eccentric, but that's only a polite word for crazy."

"I'd hardly put it as strongly as that, Judy girl. The poor man simply had too much trouble all at once. He lost everything in the world that was dear to him."

"He must live in those two locked rooms now," Judy decided. "The kitchen looked as though somebody used it but the rest of his furniture was covered up with white sheets. It looked so spooky! Did you ever hear any rumors that his house was haunted?"

"No, but I wouldn't be surprised to hear them," he replied. "He probably does do queer things, living by himself and brooding over his troubles. He probably keeps the furniture covered so that it won't remind him of his wife and daughter."

"His daughter was older than Sally, wasn't she?" Judy asked.

Dr. Bolton nodded. "She would be in her early twenties now although then she was not much older. He always thought she ran away to get married. She was a lovely ash blonde."

"What did the doctor look like, Dad? Was he tall and thin and a little stooped and did he have white hair and queer blue eyes?"

Dr. Bolton attempted to describe him but the description was vague and when he had finished, he added. "He was tall and rather stocky then, but he may have grown thin and his hair may have whitened. I couldn't say."

"Is he a relative of the Vincent's?" Judy asked, trying to connect him with her own visitor who had called himself the Vincent girl's uncle. She did wish she knew whether he was talking about Kay or Sally.

"Not a relative. As I remember it," her father said, "he was a friend and also the family's favorite specialist."

"They wouldn't have called him 'uncle' would they? I mean, the Vincent children?"

"They might have. I couldn't say. Judy, you're not eating your dinner."

She had been afraid he would notice that.

"She looks a little flushed, don't you think?" her mother asked. "Judy, are you feeling quite all right this morning?"

"I guess I caught a little cold. That's all."

"You sound hoarse," her father observed. "Right after dinner I want you to come into my office."

"But Peter is coming right after dinner," she protested, panicky for fear she'd be ordered to bed. "He and I were going down to the court-house to look at the Vincent will."

"They think maybe Sally is an heiress," Horace put in, for once taking his sister's part, "Dad, you must let Judy go."

"I will, Son—unless she is running a temperature."

Judy certainly felt uncomfortable enough to be having a fever as she followed her father to his office.

She waited, with the thermometer in her mouth, expecting it to rise to a hundred and five degrees at least. But, to her delight, it was just under ninety-nine.

"I guess I was just excited. That's why I was so flushed. Now may I go?" she asked.

"Just as soon as I look at that throat."

He looked at it, painted it with something that tasted like rusty water, and then patted her shoulder.

"All right, Judy girl, to the court house if you must. But be in bed early tonight and that's doctor's orders."

"I will," she replied. "Thank you, Dad."

And then she ran out to meet Peter who was just coming up the walk.

CHAPTER XIV

THE Farringdon courthouse was a large, impressive-looking stone building with a clock in the tower and a spacious park around it. In the park were trees, benches, a cannon which pointed toward Main Street and a soldier's monument facing Grove Street and the more fashionable shops.

Whenever she walked up the courthouse steps Judy was impressed anew with the majesty of the law. Inside was a wide hall lined with doors that announced the importance of the work going on behind them. A massive oak staircase led to the courtroom and other offices on the second floor.

Turning the knob of a door marked PROBATE, Peter escorted Judy into the room where Lou Vincent's will was filed. He asked for it at the desk and presently a clerk brought it and sat watching while they examined it at a long table. At the other end of the table was an old lady, preoccupied, writing her will. The room seemed very solemn and important to Judy. When she spoke, she felt that she must whisper.

"It's typewritten," she whispered, taking the paper in her hand. "Harry Vincent said he wasn't able to write it, but he could have dictated it, couldn't he? I really don't think they have a case against him at all."

Peter was reading the will with her.

"The form is correct," he announced. "It's just as I thought. He lists all his property— the house where Kay's family used to live in Farringdon, the factory site and, look at this, Judy! All those shabby little houses on upper Grove Street."

"They were Lou's!" she exclaimed, forgetting to whisper. "But Harry Vincent's been collecting rents and taking charge of them ever since we lived in Farringdon. He even sold the downtown house."

"He's probably temporary administrator——"

"Whatever that is," Judy interrupted. "Your legal terms confuse me. I'm afraid I don't know what a temporary administrator is."

"Well, it's this way," Peter explained. Sometimes there is a delay in probating a will. I don't know what the delay is here, but if the case were mine, I'd make it my business to find out. You know what probate is, of course?"

She laughed. "Of course. It's the sign on the glass door——"

"Seriously, Judy?"

"Well then, I don't know exactly. I should have remembered to study that pamphlet."

"It means when a will is opened and examined in an office like this and its contents are made known to the public. Sometimes, as I said, there is a delay. Then someone else is appointed to take care of the property and, as he was Lou's oldest brother, Harry Vincent was probably appointed although, according to the will, the property actually was to go to his younger brother, Ned. The profits all go back to the estate disposed of in the will. I should say it must be quite a substantial fortune."

"And Sally gets it all unless Harry Vincent wins his case?"

Peter studied the will a moment longer.

"Practically all of it," he said. "As Ned Vincent's daughter, the property should go to her."

"But what about that house below Roulsville where the Vincents live now? Would that be hers too?"

"It might be. If her father is Ned Vincent, and I'm reasonably sure he is, then he probably left it to her. That is, if she is his only child. Harry Vincent, as her guardian, might have been allowed to move in so that Sally would have a home."

"I begin to see it all," Judy said thoughtfully. "Harry Vincent is temporary administrator, guardian and everything. But I thought you said the court appoints a guardian."

"It does—a special guardian in cases like this where a child's legal rights must be protected."

"Sally needs protection all right," Judy declared, "if she has to live with Kay's family. Remember what she said about outgrown clothes? I bet she gets all Kay's hand-me-downs. No wonder she said she hoped she'd have quintuplets."

The woman, still busy with her will at the other end of the long table, looked up with a shocked expression and Judy was reminded that she was still in the solemn room where wills were filed. The clerk began tapping on the table with his pencil.

"I guess he thinks we're taking a long time," said Judy, turning to the second page of Lou Vincent's will. It was neatly typewritten, as was the first.

"There's a legacy here for Kay and Dickie," she announced presently. "I'm glad he didn't forget them altogether. It's a trust fund for their education. And now listen to this!"

Holding the paper more toward the light, she began reading in an excited voice:

"I do further give, devise and bequeath to my niece, Sally Vincent, the "emergency box" and its contents . . .

"Could that have been the box she found in our cellar?" Judy stopped to question. "No wonder she was surprised to find its contents gone! She knew about it. The will goes on to say:

"She has my instructions . . .

"But why do you suppose Lou Vincent called it 'the emergency box?' "

"There's only one reason that I can think of," Peter replied. "Its contents must have been meant to use only in case of emergency. Somebody else probably knew where it was hidden and emptied it. But, in order to do that, the person would have had to enter your house.''

"Perhaps before we lived there. This will is dated seven years ago.''

"Yes, of course,'' Peter agreed. "Vine Thompson would have gladly helped herself to anything she found hidden in the house. But I'm rather more inclined to suspect your midnight visitor.''

"Well, I'm not,'' Judy said. "You wouldn't be either if you had seen him. From his looks I'd suspect him of being a minister before I'd call him a thief. I've told you, he was gentle and kind. I think now he must have been looking for Sally because he wanted to help her.''

"A queer sort of help—scaring her half to death. But I hope you're right. She certainly needs somebody on her side of this mix-up.''

"I hope she didn't catch the same cold I did,'' said Judy, still aware of an uncomfortable dryness in her throat.

Peter turned to the last page of the will and spread the paper out on the table. There, at the bottom, just as it should be, was Lou Vincent's signature.

"It's a little shaky,'' Judy remarked.

"This will was drawn up the day before he

died,'' Peter reminded her. "And now, just take a look at the signatures of those two witnesses!''

Judy looked and her eyes grew as round as saucers.

"Dr. Burlingame!'' she exclaimed. "Do you think Sally knew it?''

"She acted as if she'd never heard of the will before. The other witness is his wife. That's bad,'' Peter commented. "The testimony of the witnesses in a case like this is very important and here one of them is dead and the other one, to say the least, is a little eccentric. I begin to see why Harry Vincent decided to contest this will.''

"Then the whole thing is a fraud!'' Judy was always quick to jump at conclusions. "Just another one of Harry Vincent's crooked schemes only this time he's cheating his own brother's little girl. I knew he was low, Peter. But I didn't think even Harry Vincent was as low as that. This case is going to be more exciting than I ever dreamed. The only sad thing about it is that it's not our case.''

"It may be,'' he told her, "if we can locate Sally. Remember those questions she asked about a special guardian?''

"Could you be her guardian, Peter?"

"Very easily," he said, rising and handing the folded will back to the clerk who had been watching them examine it. "That is, in case Sally is over fourteen—and I think she is, and again, in case she wanted me."

"Wouldn't Harry Vincent have anything to say about it?"

Peter beamed.

"No, Judy, not a single, solitary thing. And wouldn't I love to fight him in the courtroom! I can't think of anything that would please me more. As Sally's guardian, I would have the same chance to assist in the case that I would have had as Mr. Sander's assistant. The important difference would be, I'd be on the other side of the table—fighting with Sally, not against her."

"You must do it!" Judy agreed. "She needs you. I know she does. Can't we drive over there and see if she's at Harry Vincent's place this very afternoon?"

"What about your throat?" he asked. "And have you forgotten that fallen tree that is still spread full length across the garage driveway? I'm afraid the next step for me is to help Horace chop it up and haul it out of there."

"Oh, dear!" she sighed. "That will take an awfully long time, won't it?"

"Not if we keep at it, and then, if you feel all right tomorrow morning, all three of us can make the trip. We might stop off and call on Dr. Burlingame on the way. I'd rather like to meet the man who was witness to Lou Vincent's will."

"He has a funny handwriting. Burly letters, I'd call them. Can't you just picture a big man writing like this—round and bold?"

Peter laughed. "Your midnight visitor, I imagine, would have more of a ghostly hand. It might even be quite invisible."

"There may be more truth in that statement than you think," Judy exclaimed, thrusting her hand in the pocket of her navy blue jacket. "I don't suppose this will show us much more than we've seen already, but I brought along my magnifying glass."

CHAPTER XV

JUDY's magnifying glass had been useful to her several times before when baffling mysteries had come up for her to solve. Once, by peering through it, she had discovered a singed edge of paper that turned out to be a clue to the fire that destroyed the girls' High School in Farringdon. The school had since been rebuilt and Judy had graduated only a year ago. It seemed longer, for so much had happened. But she remembered the fire well. She also remembered the prize poster contest. Kay Vincent had tried to cheat, just as Judy expected her father was doing now. She looked more closely at his brother's signature.

"It's even more shaky through the glass," she observed. "And look how it goes uphill. That's supposed to stand for something, but I've forgotten what. His signature isn't half as clear as Dr. Burlingame's or Mrs. Burlingame's either. She had a typically feminine hand."

143

"They were all three signed with the same pen or, at least, with the same kind of ink," Peter said, after taking a turn with the magnifying glass. The clerk at the table was watching closely.

"Is that important?" asked Judy.

"It might help prove that Lou Vincent signed his will in the presence of witnesses. We'll need to prove that." He broke off and Judy realized that he hadn't meant to talk as though the case were already his. But she had never seen him more interested.

"I wish we had a sample of Ned Vincent's handwriting here to compare the two," Judy said. "They'll try to prove that Ned signed this. Two brothers could easily have similar handwriting, couldn't they? Lou's isn't very individual, do you think?"

"I'm afraid I couldn't qualify as a handwriting expert," laughed Peter. "Judy Bolton, *what are you doing?*"

She had turned again to the second page of the will and was holding it toward the light, then tilting it away and squinting at it through the magnifying glass. The clerk was watching more suspiciously than ever.

"I think something's been written here and

then erased," she announced. "I'm just trying to make out what it is."

Peter rose to his feet excitedly, then peered at the will over her shoulder.

"Are you sure there's an erasure? That's important," he declared. "According to law, a will stands as it was first written."

"You mean that whatever was erased is still a part of the will?"

"That's right. It still stands. That is, if the hidden writing can be determined."

"I'm doing my best," Judy told him, tilting the paper at a new angle. "Talk about a ghostly hand! This might easily be spirit writing for all I can see of it."

"It isn't a hand when it's typewritten. And ghosts don't use typewriters," joked Peter. Then he added, more seriously, as he studied the portion of the will that she had indicated, "It is a little rough."

Judy touched it with her finger and the clerk immediately rose and made an objection. It was his duty to see that none of the wills in his keeping were marked or defaced by the slightest touch.

"I guess I can't point it out to you," she said ruefully, "but you see, right after it says 'she has my instructions' something was typed in and then rubbed out again. There's no period after the word 'instructions' but there is an erased period about half an inch farther on."

"Let me have a look at it."

Peter took the paper and screwed up his eyes into small slits, squinting at it.

"I think there's an X in the center," Judy pointed out, "but what word with an X in it could be written in half an inch of space and have any possible meaning?"

"It might be X-ray. Something in an X-ray picture. But I don't see how an X-ray picture could instruct anybody as to the whereabouts of a box."

"But the X is in the center. If you hold it in this light . . ." She tilted the paper a little more toward the window. "There, now can you see it?"

"Very faintly. Maybe he gave her the instructions in Texas," said Peter, half-joking.

"Or near some exit. That wouldn't be definite, though, just to say 'she has my instructions exit.' "

"Sort of daffy, if you ask me. Perhaps it says 'she has my instructions exactly.' "

"No, Peter, there isn't room for a seven-letter

word. You see, there are only five spaces. No, it isn't that.''

"Could it have been axe? That reminds me. Horace and I still have that tree to chop up for firewood. You can puzzle this out at home while you watch us.''

"I shan't want to watch you. Peter,'' she asked, ''suppose we can't make it out at all. What will we do then?''

"Tell the clerk, of course. He suspects there's something wrong already.''

"But what can he do?''

"Submit it to the Court to decide why and when the erasure was made. Under proper supervision the paper could be moistened and a special kind of powder sifted over it to bring out the hidden writing. It works something the same as determining finger prints.''

Judy glanced at the little owl-eyed man whose business it was to watch them as they examined the will.

"I think we're being properly supervised this very minute,'' she said. ''Couldn't we get some of that powder you mentioned and do it ourselves?''

"I'm afraid not,'' he said soberly. ''You're forgetting that this is not our case.''

With that he rose and handed the folded will back to the clerk.

"There's an erasure on this," he commented. "The Court may want to look into it more thoroughly."

Immediately the clerk was all interest. Peter pointed it out but, at first, the clerk's nearsighted eyes failed to see it. The space between the word "instructions" and the almost obliterated period finally convinced him.

"By Jove, it is an erasure!" he ejaculated. "Thank you, sir. Will you step over here to the desk, sir?"

"Gladly," he replied, throwing Judy a meaning smile.

She waited while Peter and several other men gathered excitedly around a large desk at the far corner of the room. This desk was separated from the long tables by a railing and back of it were shelves to the ceiling. On the shelves were fat law books. One of the men took down several of them and handed one to Peter. He looked up something and there was more excited talk before he finally came back to Judy.

"We've stirred up some interest in the case, at least," he remarked as they left the room and began descending the wide oak stairway.

"What was it you asked them? I mean,"
Judy explained, "when they got out all those
big books and acted so excited."

"I asked them how it was that probate of this
will had been delayed so long."

"And what did they say?"

"They said," stated Peter in a quiet voice,
just as though he were conveying some less
startling information, "that after a person is
missing for seven years under circumstances
which afford reasonable ground for believing he
is dead, his will may be probated even though
there is no actual proof of his death."

"And that, translated," cried Judy, "means
that Lou Vincent may still be alive! Peter, we
must meet Dr. Burlingame and, if I find out that
he wasn't my midnight visitor, then I'll know
that Lou Vincent was!"

"Just a minute! Just a minute!" Peter
stopped her. "Before we risk our necks calling
on a man who may be a dangerous lunatic, don't
you think it might be a good idea to look up the
facts of Lou Vincent's death in the old newspaper files?"

"Of course," she agreed. "Horace can find
them for us in a minute and the *Herald* office is
just across the street."

CHAPTER XVI

It took quite some time to hunt up the old newspapers that carried the story of Lou Vincent's accident and later his supposed death. Horace met Judy and Peter in what was called the *Herald's* morgue and helped them search.

Horace was familiar with the morgue and the heavy, bound files filled with newspapers for at least fifty years back. The Farringdon *Daily Herald* had started as a little county weekly when a great portion of the county was nothing but unsettled wilderness. It had grown, with the town, and here in the room full of old files was its history.

Choosing a file dated seven years ago, Horace began turning the pages. Every so often Judy or Peter stopped him to glance at some especially interesting piece of news or to laugh at the department store advertisements with the queer old styles. One of the long waisted dresses shown was like the dress Sally had been wearing when they found her.

150

"Isn't it funny," remarked Judy, "that girls' dresses get queer so soon and men's clothes always stay the same?"

"Men don't like fancy do-dads," said Horace importantly as he turned another page.

Judy grabbed his wrist, trembling with excitement.

"Look, Horace! It's an account of Lou's accident. Peter, look at this!"

She pointed out the headline: THREE MEN INJURED IN EXPLOSION.

It had happened, they discovered, in a polishing plant connected with the furniture factory that the Vincent brothers owned. The factory itself was just across the valley from Judy's home. The polishing plant had been nearer. Judy recognized it from the picture in the old newspaper as the ugly, black building that used to stand just across the street from the house where the Brady family now lived. The building, to her great relief, had recently been torn down. She had always disliked passing it late in the evening.

"So that was the old, broken-down factory that used to be such an eye-sore!" she exclaimed. "No wonder it had such a sinister look about it. It was partly burned, this account says, and then it lists the men who were injured. Lou Vincent was one of them.''

She began reading aloud from the paper.

''He was rushed to Dr. Burlingame's office where he was treated for burns and shock. The doctor stated that his condition was serious, refusing to make further comment.''

''Even then,'' remarked Peter, ''it seems he wasn't very talkative.''

''Or else he had something to conceal,'' Judy put in excitedly. ''You remember, Harry Vincent said he was burned with inflammable furniture polish shortly before he died. He didn't say he died of his burns though. And Marge said there was some quarrel. It's all very queer, isn't it?''

''Queerer than that,'' agreed Horace. ''I don't wonder that people have been seeing ghosts.''

''There must be another account either of his death or his disappearance,'' Peter put in.

''I'm looking for it,'' Judy told him, turning over the pages of the old file and scanning each column of newsprint very carefully. She stopped to read an account of another accident and Horace became impatient with her.

''You can't read the whole paper, you know.

We haven't got all day. That's an auto accident and has nothing to do with the explosion.''

Judy turned on him, her gray eyes dark with excitement.

''Doesn't it? Well then, read it for yourself!''

All three of them now bent eagerly over the article. The headlines ran:

CAR CRASHES OVER EMBANKMENT
Two Occupants Feared Dead

Roulsville, April 8th. A car operated by Ray Suffern of Farringdon crashed over a twenty foot embankment into the muddy waters of Roulsville Run some time yesterday afternoon. With the young man when the accident occurred, was his employer, Lou Vincent . . .

''Suffering Tom Cats!'' ejaculated Peter. ''It was an automobile accident that finished him? Now why have the Vincents kept that so dark?''

''Read on and you may see,'' Judy told him. ''Naturally, they didn't want the general public to know there was any doubt as to whether or not he was still alive.''

''It doesn't look to me as though there was much of any,'' Horace put in. ''They crashed down a twenty foot embankment, didn't they? And Lou Vincent was already severely burned.''

Judy studied the picture beside the article. It was marked with a white cross where the car had left the road. The tire marks and the broken bushes at the left were clearly shown in the photograph. It certainly looked as though both Lou and his companion must have been instantly killed.

"I know right where this accident happened," she announced, turning to Peter. "Remember that high bank just as we came out of Roulsville? It has a whitewashed fence with metal ropes between the posts to keep cars from crashing over now but when I think of us driving through there yesterday when you could hardly see, Peter, it chills me! This whole account is a little too gruesome!"

The newspaper article went on to tell how the river was flooded, making search for the bodies difficult. The car was completely submerged.

"And that," said Horace, "is all you're likely to find out until we see Dr. Burlingame. Lou's only chance was that he might have jumped and, of course, if he was as badly burned as we are led to suppose, that would have been impossible."

"Dr. Burlingame can tell us that, can't he?" asked Judy.

"If he'll tell us anything," Peter replied doubtfully. "I must confess, I don't like the idea of taking a girl on a trip like that."

"It's taking a chance all right," Horace agreed. "You and I could go over there to-gether as soon as we get the car out——"

"Look here, you two!" Judy interrupted, fac-ing them belligerently. "Do you believe in equal rights or don't you? Well then, if you do, I'm taking that trip too. How are you going to identify Dr. Burlingame if I'm not along? You didn't see our midnight visitor. Besides, even if you're right and he is a little bit crazy, a woman's wiles might easily avail against a man's brute strength."

"Listen to her!" grinned Peter. "She thinks she's got wiles."

"Well, I've got something," she declared, "or I wouldn't have been able to solve all those other mysteries."

"You've got a sore throat," Horace reminded her, "and you promised Dad you'd take care of it."

"Well, if it gets better," Peter conceded at last, "she may as well go. We can't start until tomorrow morning at the earliest. I intend to see this doctor and then call on Harry Vincent."

"Wherever we go," laughed Judy, "I doubt if we'll be very welcome. Horace, just how does one go about seeing people who don't want to be seen?"

While they walked home he explained some of his methods. A good reporter always has a few tricks for getting into places where he isn't supposed to be. Horace usually managed it by edging in behind some taller person or pretending to be a member of some group with which he was not really connected. But these tricks could not be worked this time. Peter and Horace and Judy were all the group there was.

"How about chopping up that tree and getting it out of the way this afternoon?" Peter asked when they came in sight of the Bolton house. There were still several trees in the spacious yard but Judy was conscious of a gap where her favorite shade tree had stood. The upturned roots reminded her of a giant octopus heaved out of the sea.

"Speaking of equal rights," Horace said. "Judy also has a right to help us chop up the tree."

"No, thank you," she replied. "I think I prefer to follow doctor's orders and lie down for a while."

"You must be sick——"

"Not at all," she interrupted. "I feel fine But I intend to keep on feeling that way. You know, I'm taking that trip with you tomorrow."

Upstairs, as she lay on her bed trying to take a late afternoon nap, Judy could hear the boys at work on the tree. The saw Horace was using had a mournful sound as if it were repeating, "Ah, me! Ah, me!" Downstairs in his cage, the parrot was trying to imitate it, the result being something between a squawk and a moan.

Peter swung his axe with a more cheerful *chop! chop!* But even that was like a cry from the heart of the tree that had shaded Judy's home. She wondered if her midnight visitor had seen it fall and again she asked herself whether he had really been there. Well, tomorrow she'd know. It might be a good idea to ask Dr. Burlingame about the hidden writing on the will as well.

It had become a habit with Judy to save the clues to all her mysteries in some visible form. The X she had deciphered from the will was a clue and, consequently, ought to be recorded and saved. Although she had not slept, she decided she had rested long enough and got up again. Tearing a slip of paper off the pad on her desk, she wrote a large X on it and opened her clue drawer.

There, on top of the reminders of past mysteries, was a very present reminder of something that had happened only the night before. It was the slip of paper she had found in Sally's pocket:

$$7 \times 7$$

"There's my answer!" cried Judy, catching up Blackberry and hugging him, since there was no one else in the room to share her excitement. "It wasn't an X at all. It was a times sign!"

Yes, she felt certain that was right. The times sign just fit—seven and a space, times and a space, and then seven again. That made exactly five spaces. There was just room for 7×7 to have been typewritten after the statement, "She has my instructions." In the original will it must have read, "She has my instructions 7×7."

Thrilled by her discovery, Judy raced downstairs and out the front door. Peter and Horace looked up from their chopping.

"I've solved the hidden writing!" she cried, waving both slips of paper. "It's seven times seven—the same as the paper in Sally's pocket. Now let's try and solve that."

CHAPTER XVII

THE EMPTY HIDING PLACE

By EIGHT o'clock that evening the tree was reduced to a pile of substantial chunks which would burn cheerfully in the fireplace all winter. One by one, Horace and Peter lugged them down cellar and stored them in a far corner beyond the work-bench.

"Look carefully and don't put them on top of anything," Judy warned them. "There are still a few unsolved mysteries down cellar."

She followed them, still carrying the two slips of paper around with her, just as though there were the least possibility of forgetting the significant 7×7.

"I'm sure it marks the place where the 'emergency box' was kept," she said.

Horace grunted, putting down a heavy chunk. Then he rubbed his arms.

"Good for the muscles," he observed. "Just as soon as this job's done, Sis, we'll help you look."

"Judy!" called her mother from upstairs. "You're not down cellar again with that sore throat?"

"It isn't sore any more, Mother."

"It will be if you expose yourself to all that dampness. I noticed you didn't eat your dinner any too well. Come on up!"

"I'm coming," Judy replied listlessly. It was nice, she thought, to have people caring about you and thinking of your health. But at times it was something of a nuisance.

"Seven times seven," she kept repeating to herself.

It might be seven feet along the tunnel. But what would the other seven stand for? Suppose you took seven steps from the foot of the cellar stairs and then turned and walked seven more steps toward the wall. Steps weren't all the same. People measured things by feet or by paces. The living room was warm enough. Nobody would mind if she walked in there and looked up "pace" in the dictionary.

The result was not very satisfying—"a step in walking; a measure in length, usually three feet." Well, seven times three was twenty-one. That would be twenty-one feet one way and twenty-one feet the other. Or it might simply be seven feet one way and seven feet another.

"Mother, may I just go down cellar for a minute and measure something?" she asked.

"If you must, dear. But come right up."

Thankfully, Judy took a yard stick and, with Blackberry following as always, went down the cellar stairs once more. She'd wear them thin if this kept up.

Her cat watched her curiously; then, supposing the yard stick to be meant for him to play with, made a dart toward it. The yard stick moved and Judy had to begin all over again. Her measurements brought her just to the edge of the coal bin. The floor there was hard and flat. She swept away the gravel and found nothing but packed dirt underneath. Blackberry tilted his nose disdainfully when she attempted to make him sniff at it. Often he found things for her but this time his manner said plainly that there was nothing to find.

"I guess it wasn't paces," she told him and began measuring the floor in feet. This time she ended up within an inch of the furnace and again found nothing.

"It's no use, Blackberry. It wasn't feet either," she decided and, holding him, returned to the living room.

"Your father wants you to go to bed early," Mrs. Bolton reminded her.

"But Mother, I did nap—" she began and then remembered that she hadn't really. She had only lay on her bed for a half hour or so puzzling over the mystery and then thought of writing down the clue. Then had come the discovery. It wasn't what she dared call a nap.

Horace and Peter came in looking like a couple of lumber jacks. Horace declared his hands were full of splinters.

"I don't envy the old-timers who had to chop all their own wood," he said. "I prefer chopping newspaper stories to pieces and that," he added, "is usually what happens to them."

"I wonder if anybody chopped up those stories we were looking at this afternoon," Judy said. "There was plenty we didn't find out."

"For one day's work," Peter told her, "I think we all made a pretty good job of finding out things."

Turning to Mrs. Bolton, he then began recounting the day's adventures, telling her what they had learned about Lou Vincent in the old newspaper files and how Judy had discovered the hidden writing on the will and compared it with the note in Sally's pocket.

"And now, Judy," he finished, "we're ready to start hunting."

Mrs. Bolton sighed and put down her sewing.

"What is it you're trying to find this time?" she inquired.

They all looked at each other blankly.

"Well," Horace said at last, "what is it?"

"Seven up and seven down or seven out and seven in of something and when we find it we won't know what it is," Peter informed her.

"Just as clear as mud, isn't it, Mother?" laughed Judy. "Well, I have it figured out a little better than that. The secret cellar has a stone wall. Now suppose you count seven stones from the tunnel and seven stones up from the floor. Where would that bring you?"

"To another stone," Horace suggested logically.

"Exactly," she retorted. "But couldn't there be something hidden behind that stone?"

"By jinks, there could!" ejaculated Peter, grabbing her hand. "Come on, let's look."

"Put a scarf around your neck if you must go down cellar again," Mrs. Bolton cautioned her.

Taking that as consent, Judy and the two boys trooped eagerly down the stairs again.

"I guess it's okay," she told them. "But I can't stay down here very long. Mother's right. The dampness down here may hurt my throat and I wouldn't miss that trip tomorrow for anything."

"The secret cellar is probably fairly dry by now, thanks to you," Peter remarked as he threw open the trap door and they began descending the ladder.

Their voices had an odd, hollow sound once they were all beneath the floor. The upper cellar had never been cemented but it was covered with gravel which served almost as well. But here the floor was dirt and nothing else. The farther wall, also, was of packed, brown earth. It had been hollowed out into a fairly good-sized room at first and then, where the stone wall ended, it narrowed into the tunnel. Only two sides of the cellar were built of stone and it was these that Judy had described.

"You try that side and I'll try this one," Peter directed Horace. "These stones would be pretty heavy, Judy, if they should be loose. You had better leave it to us."

"Gladly," she replied, "but I don't know which one of you to watch."

At first Horace thought his stone yielded a

little, but it was only a loose piece of mortar. The work of building this cellar had probably been done very hurriedly.

"You might as well try to lift the house," he said at last, giving it up.

Meanwhile Peter had been patiently prodding the opposite stone until now he was sure he had loosened it a little.

"But how Sally could have lifted a stone this size is beyond me," he began and then, breaking off suddenly, shouted, "Watch out!" and jumped to one side.

The stone that had fallen was square and flat. It hadn't been meant to fit all the way into the opening behind it. For there, before their astonished eyes, was a hiding place big enough for a much larger box than the one Sally had discovered. And now they felt fairly certain she had found it here.

Judy lifted the flat stone. "It isn't heavy at all," she remarked. "It's like a little door."

With his hand all the way into the opening, Peter felt around, finding nothing.

"Let me try it," urged Judy, standing on tiptoe.

Her hand was smaller. Reaching in as far as she could, she discovered that the hollow place behind the small, flat stone extended a little to the right. It probably met the small space that must be behind the solid stone beside it.

"I don't suppose there's anything there," she said doubtfully, "but if you boys feel like tugging at another stone, at least, we might look."

Horace was skeptical.

"If you found the real hiding place empty, what makes you think a tiny space that wasn't even supposed to be there would have anything in it?"

"Because something might have slipped in by accident," she retorted. "Help me and I'll move the stone myself."

But they would not hear of it. Together, Horace and Peter tugged until the mortar cracked. Then Judy brought them a hammer and chisel and they pried and pounded.

"I'm warning you," Horace said with a dark look. He had just pounded his finger instead of the stone. "If something doesn't turn up this time, the search is off."

"Agreed," said Judy, watching them as they lifted the heavy stone and set it on the floor.

"There you are! See anything?"

Judy looked, but to her great disappointment, there was nothing in the small space that had been behind the stone—nothing but caked brown dirt, damp and musty-smelling, exactly like that in the floor of the secret cellar.

"Satisfied, Judy?" they asked. "Shall we put it back?"

She sighed. "I'm satisfied. We looked for nothing and found nothing and it was just about what I expected."

They had forgotten Blackberry, romping about on the dirt floor. But just as they were about to leave, Judy noticed that he was playing with a tiny slip of yellowed paper. How he had gotten it, she had no idea. But it was just possible that it had fallen from the hiding place.

"Blackberry, give it up!" she ordered, stroking his head and unloosening the paper carefully from his claw.

"What is it?" asked Peter.

"A piece of paper. But there's some writing on it. Look!"

In the same uncertain hand with which he had signed the will, Lou Vincent had written a note, apparently intending it to be found by Sally.

Forgive me. It was an emergency.
                              Uncle Lou

CHAPTER XVIII

A CHANGE OF PLANS

THE first thing Judy did when she arose the following morning was to look in her clue drawer and make sure the note in Lou Vincent's handwriting was still there. It was hard to believe they had really found it and harder still not to be a little awed by the significance of such a note. As she studied it, a plan that had been forming in her mind took definite shape.

"I will take it along," she decided, slipping the note in the zipper compartment of her pocketbook.

Downstairs she found Horace and Peter all ready to start on the trip. They were a little impatient that she had kept them waiting.

"How do you feel this morning?" Horace asked suspiciously.

"Never better," she replied, seating herself at the table. "Did you boys have some of these delicious corn muffins?"

Horace confessed that he had eaten several.

Peter, who had breakfasted earlier with his grandparents and his sister Honey, agreed to try one. Honey had wanted to come on the trip but he had discouraged her.

"One girl is enough to take," he explained briefly.

Judy smiled. They might be taking only one, but if her plan worked as she hoped it would, they might be bringing home two—herself and Sally.

"I'm packing the rest of these corn muffins and a box of fig newtons for us to lunch on in case we're tied up somewhere," she announced, filling a paper bag.

"You must expect something to happen——"

"I expect plenty to happen," she replied, "and I intend to be prepared for it."

Peter had cleaned the car. Considering its age, it looked quite presentable. It was a small car but in the rear was a rather large compartment for trunks, suitcases or whatever Peter wished to carry. Judy felt that a machine gun might come in handy, but the compartment was empty except for the small bag of lunch which seemed almost lost in one corner. Closing the lid, Judy climbed in the front seat between Horace and Peter.

"I've changed my mind," she said, trying to sound casual, "we're not going to call on Dr. Burlingame on the way to Harry Vincent's. We're going to call on him on the way back home."

Both boys looked startled.

"But Judy, I had intended to stop off at the office and put in a little time there," Peter protested.

"I doubt if you'll want to. You'll have something more important to do by then. Please, Peter!"

"Well, you must have figured out something," he conceded doubtfully.

"When Judy changes her mind," Horace put in, "it usually means that everybody else is supposed to change his mind too. I suppose it's something about that note?"

"No," she admitted. "The note is just as puzzling as ever. I brought it along, by the way. It was meant for Sally and I intend to show it to her. She expected to find something in the emergency box and this note explains why it wasn't there. Lou Vincent took it."

"Took what?" asked Horace, still confused by the vague message in the note they had found.

"Whatever was there," she replied. "I don't

know, of course, but Sally will. That's why I
want to call on Harry Vincent first.''

"You're pretty sure that Sally is there, aren't
you?''

"Practically positive," she replied, "but I'm
equally positive we won't be permitted to see
her. You boys had better be thinking up a few
stunts. If we see her at all—and we will," she
added confidently, "we'll have to see her without permission.''

They were well on their way now. Horace
had been rumpling up his hair in his charac-
teristic fashion, trying to think, as they drove
on along the road toward Roulsville.

"This doesn't make sense to me," he spoke
up at last. "A dead man returns, helps himself
to the contents of a box, leaves a note that, somehow is discovered in a cat's claws, scares a few
people, kidnaps a girl—why it's preposterous!''

"The way you put it," said Judy, laughing,
"it certainly is.''

"I suppose you have a better solution?''

"I haven't any at all," she confessed. "I'm
just trying to find one. That's why we're calling
on Harry Vincent first. If Sally was kid-
napped, as you put it, he did the kidnapping.
Furthermore, just because we found a note in

Lou Vincent's handwriting, there's no reason for thinking that he had to return to write it. The paper was yellow and old. He could easily have written it seven years ago but, if he did, it was after he made his will.''

"That's right," Peter agreed. "Otherwise the emergency box wouldn't have been mentioned."

"The accident happened the day after he made his will," Horace put in. "Are you trying to tell me that during that twenty-four hours Lou Vincent entered our house—though, of course, it wasn't ours then—left this note and took whatever was in the emergency box?''

"I'm only saying he might have. Dr. Burlingame can tell us how badly he was hurt in the explosion. I'd like to take Sally with us when we go to see him."

"If you hadn't been right so often in the past," Peter declared, "I'd agree with Horace that this is utter nonsense. In the first place, Sally may not be at Harry Vincent's. In the second place, we may not be able to see her if she is. And in the third place, I don't believe she'll be willing to return with us, especially if she knows we're stopping off at that spooky Burlingame house. She was glad enough to get away from it before. Why should we take her back there?''

"Dr. Burlingame," said Judy, "is our most important witness and don't you dare tell me, Peter Dobbs, that this is not our case."

"Well, it isn't," he began and then, seeing the look she gave him, closed his lips tightly and turned his attention to his driving.

The road ahead wound up a hill in a number of S curves; then down again into Dry Brook Hollow where Judy's grandparents had their farm. Often Judy and Peter stopped off to greet them on their way to and from the office. Sometimes they stayed for a good country dinner. But this time they only hailed Red, the boy who worked the farm, and drove on.

"It's along here somewhere that Lou must have had his accident," Judy observed as they neared Roulsville. "See! The streams join just across the valley and then the road goes for a little distance along the bank just above Roulsville Run. There!" She pointed. "See the row of posts. That must be the place."

They rounded another curve and suddenly the river was right below them, muddy and high after the storm, just as it must have been on that April day seven years before. Peter slowed down only a moment while all three of them tried to imagine the accident. It was too much for Judy.

"Let's drive on," she said. "There's no use looking at it."

"Lou Vincent is dead all right," said Horace grimly. "No car could crash over that bank without killing every soul in it."

They were all inclined to agree with him. Judy felt a vague sadness about it all. She could not put his message from her mind. *Forgive me. It was an emergency.* But he couldn't have known about the accident ahead of time.

In Roulsville Peter stopped off just long enough to see if there was anything for him at the office. He read his mail, decided that none of the letters demanded immediate answers, and climbed back into the car. He now turned down the south road that went toward Harry Vincent's recently acquired dwelling.

They passed a few farms and then came to South Roulsville as it used to be called. It was now known by the more distinctive name of South Park. The dwellings here had not been touched by the Roulsville flood. By the time the waters had reached this extreme end of the valley they had lost their fury. A bridge had been washed out, a few fields flooded, but the buildings still stood as stately and majestic as ever. Most of them were set far back from the road and surrounded by trees.

"This must be Harry Vincent's place," Peter remarked as he slowed down before a large stone house with towers.

"Don't stop!" Judy cautioned him. "We can't go right in, you know. I thought perhaps if we circled the drive and then took a turn around that other road to the back we might attract Sally's attention. It's Sally we want to see, not Harry Vincent."

"There's sense in that," Peter agreed, guiding the car as she had directed and finally stopping beside a tall hedge at the back of the house. This was a private roadway to the next estate, but so far nobody appeared to have noticed the car drive in.

"There isn't a sign of life about the place," Judy observed, anxiously watching the back windows. She had hoped to see Sally's face in one of them. But the whole aspect of Harry Vincent's house was as dismal as a church yard. She thought of calling. Sally might hear her call—but so would the others.

"Whistle to her, Peter," she suggested.

He whistled—a long, shrill note like a bird. Still nothing happened.

Horace added one of his inimitable cat-calls and a dog barked somewhere in the direction of the house.

"We're announced," he said, turning to the others. All three of them were now standing just behind the hedge. "We might as well ring the door bell now. Mrs. Vincent or one of the maids might answer it. They might not know how dangerous we are," he added, grinning broadly.

"We could try it," Judy agreed. "But there's no use going all the way around to the front again. We can squeeze through this opening in the hedge."

Peter went first and Judy followed, catching her hair in the thorns. It was a barberry hedge like the one around the Farringdon-Pett house. A blue jay squawked and Judy caught a glimpse of his beautiful tufted head and shining wings as he flew away.

Again the dog barked. They could see him now, a funny little white terrier jumping about on the side lawn and making a great deal of noise. But the moment Judy spoke to him he stopped barking and began wagging his tail.

"Good doggie!" she said. "Find Sally."

He trotted toward the house and they followed. There was no way out of it now. They had been announced several times.

The porch was screened in with a bell outside the screen. While the dog waited expectantly, Peter pressed it. Inside the house they heard the sound of chimes.

"It's pretty, isn't it? I like it better than the shrill bell we have," Judy said. "But it isn't very loud. I wonder if they can hear it."

"They can certainly hear this dog," Peter assured her.

He was scratching and whining at the door. Finally he set up a series of little howls.

"It's no use, doggie," said Judy, patting his head. "I guess they're not at home."

"Well, there's no point in simply standing here—" Horace began. But just then a board creaked and they heard the sound of light footsteps inside the house. Presently the door opened and there stood Kay.

"Judy Bolton!" she exclaimed just as though she were delighted to see her. "My dear! This is a pleasure. I meant to ask you down some time. And the boys too! Come right in."

CHAPTER XIX

KAY VINCENT had changed very little since Judy last saw her. The sleek brown hair that used to be set in precise waves was now combed to the back of her head in precise curls. But the girl's face was just as hard and her lips just as thin and unlovely as ever. They followed her into the entrance hall while she continued talking.

"I'm so sorry I had to run away from your party, Judy. I'm sure it must have been delightful. I came back later, you know, just in time to find that funny little cousin of mine running out into the rain. The next day Father told me you had called up and were worried about her——"

"Where is she now?" Judy interrupted, finding her voice after that first moment of stunned surprise. The honey sweet tone of Kay's voice had not deceived her. She might or might not be telling the truth.

178

"Yes, where is she?" Horace repeated when Kay hesitated. "Your father was right. Judy was worried and so were all the rest of us."

"Sally has a habit of worrying people, I'm afraid," Kay said condescendingly. "She shouldn't have accepted that dress you gave her. We're always buying her things. In fact, she's in Farringdon with Mother this very minute probably buying out Brandt's Department store."

Judy's eyes narrowed. That certainly didn't sound like the truth.

The dog had come in with them and was now sitting at Judy's feet. He lifted his head and pricked up his ears. There were footsteps upstairs. If Sally were in the house she would certainly hear them talking.

"That's the maid," Kay said sweetly. "Shall I have her bring you some tea?"

Judy didn't trust herself to answer but she heard Peter refusing for her. This grown-up, polite Kay was even more exasperating than the Kay who had made her so miserable in school, who had stormed at her, "You couldn't keep anything clean . . . anyone that would live in Vine Thompson's dirty house!" The two or three years in between had not erased that hurt.

Judy had stormed back at Kay then, but now she could say nothing.

"I suppose you would like to see my father," Kay said at last, turning to Peter.

"Why, yes," he replied. "I would like to see him. There may have been some mistake about that case."

He meant that, Judy knew. The mistake was when he first considered having Harry Vincent for a client.

"Oh, I'm sure there was a mistake," Kay replied, still in her affected manner. "Father was probably a little abrupt over the telephone because Judy called at such an unusual hour." She emphasized the word "unusual" with a slight inflection.

"It was all a little unusual, if you ask me," Judy spoke up. "We found your cousin scared half to death in a deserted house. Naturally, we took her home with us and again, quite naturally, when she disappeared, we were worried. We went all over the house calling, 'Sally! Sally! Sally!' "

"It's no use calling her now," said Kay, her voice not quite as sweet as it had been before. "I told you she had gone shopping with Mother."

Judy had called purposefully. The footsteps she had heard were coming down the stairs now but Kay had been right. It was only the maid. She whispered something in her ear and then went out again.

"Will you excuse me a moment?" Kay began.

"We're going now anyway," the boys told her. "Be sure to tell your father."

"I'll tell him——"

"No doubt you will," Judy interrupted. "And tell Sally too *if she really is out shopping.*"

"I'll tell her. Goodbye, Judy! *So* glad you came."

When they were safely out of hearing distance, Judy turned to Peter her gray eyes quite green.

"Couldn't you just wring her neck?"

"Quite cheerfully," he replied. "I'd forgotten how sweet a snake could be."

"Dripping honey—and poison," Horace added. "Can't you just hear her next week on the witness stand?"

"I can hear the whole nest of them—vipers, not Vincents. I wish I'd had sense enough to throw that case in Harry Vincent's face when he first mentioned it."

Judy faced him. "Now Peter, you know you don't wish that," she said. "You don't want to throw the case in his face. You want to fight back and that's exactly what we're going to do."

Running feet sounded behind them and Judy turned.

"It's Kay," she said. "What do you suppose she wants now?"

It was Kay herself who told them what she wanted although, like everything else she had said that day, it was hard to believe.

"I thought I'd see you off," she announced coming over to the car and standing beside it. "I suppose you know you're parked in our neighbor's driveway."

"How careless of us!" Peter exclaimed in mock surprise.

They had returned to the car the long way deciding that it might be just as well if Kay didn't know they had come in through an opening in the hedge.

"Picnicking?" she asked. "There are some lovely spots around here——"

"We'll find them, thank you!"

Kay still stood with her foot on the running board.

"I don't see any picnic baskets."

"Would you like to inspect the car?" asked Peter, throwing open the door. "I'm sure you won't find anything but a bag of lunch in the rear compartment."

"No, thank you," she answered, still smiling as she backed away. "Really, I hope you didn't think I was being rude. You know, Peter, you and Judy and Horace are always welcome. Come back again some time, won't you?"

"We may take you up on that," said Peter, starting the car. "That," he continued, turning to Judy, "is what I call wasting a whole morning. The trip to Dr. Burlingame's will be another time killer. He won't see us either. Harry Vincent has this whole case fixed up to suit himself. What do you say, Judy, we go back to the office and answer the letters that came this morning? Somebody may drop in. You never can tell."

Judy didn't blame him for feeling discouraged. But they mustn't give up as easily as that. They were now well out of the fashionable South Park settlement and entering a little stretch of woods.

"Judy!" Horace spoke up suddenly. "Did I hear somebody calling you?"

She looked around. The back seat of the car was empty, of course. She must be hearing things. It had sounded like a faint, "Judy! Judy!"

"Peter," she said. "You'd better stop the car. First I see a ghost and now Horace and I are both hearing voices. Instead of going back to the office we ought to stop off at the insane asylum and have our heads examined."

"You'll be all the better company for Dr. Burlingame," Peter began.

"Judy! Judy!" the call persisted.

Peter jammed on the brakes.

"Judy! Judy! Let me out!"

"It's back there where you put the lunch!" exclaimed Horace and, in one leap, he was out of the car. Judy and Peter followed, hardly knowing what to expect. Peter threw open the lid and there was Sally.

"Oh, thank you!" she gasped. "I was almost smothered."

Her head popped up as cheerfully as a jack-in-the-box. Incredibly, she was smiling.

"Sally!" they cried. "Is it really you? How did you ever get in the back of our car?"

Almost falling over each other in their eagerness, they helped her out and stood her on the ground where they could look at her. It was still hard to believe they had actually found her.

"I thought that was your whistle, Peter," she said. "You whistled like that when we were playing Murder and Horace made those funny cat calls. I've tried this stunt before and it always works."

"What stunt?" asked Judy, too surprised to follow what she was saying.

"Hiding in cars. It isn't very comfortable though," she confessed, "and it's a nuisance not knowing where you're going. This time I didn't care much so long as Peter was driving. I knew I could make you hear me as soon as you stopped the car."

"But how did you get there in the first place?"

She laughed. "Oh, that was easy. I sneaked out the back way just as you came up on the porch. Nobody saw me on account of the hedge and so I lifted up the lid and simply crawled in. Woofer kept barking and at first they didn't miss me. Kay suspected something later. That's why she followed you back to the car. When Peter said, 'Would you like to inspect it?' I nearly died. But I didn't make a peep."

"Brave little Sally! But she said you were shopping with her mother."

"Pooh!" the girl replied. "Her mother was right in the house. I guess Kay thought she was watching me and she thought Kay was. I'm watched like a mouse, you know. But you didn't know, did you? How did you find out where I was? Whatever did you think when I disappeared from your party?"

"We still don't know what to think. Come into the back seat of the car with me and tell me about it," Judy urged. "You must be dreadfully cramped after being all doubled up in there with the lunch."

"May I have some?" she asked.

"Always hungry, aren't you? Don't they feed you at the Vincent's?"

"I can't eat with people who hate me."

"We like you." Judy gave her a sudden, impulsive hug. "Oh, Sally!" she cried. "I can't tell you how good it is to have you with us again. We've imagined all sorts of things. Here, cuddle up!"

Although it was a warm day, Judy pulled a blanket over her, remembering the chill of that night in the storm. It was a miracle that Sally wasn't sick in bed. "Weak little me," she thought, "to catch such a cold when Sally could go through all this and come up smiling."

They rode along in silence for a while. Judy's heart was too full of thankfulness for her to speak.

"What happened at the party?" she asked at last. "Kay said you ran away."

"Well, I didn't," Sally declared, sitting up straight and looking directly at Judy. "I was just playing like the rest of you when Kay came in and pulled me toward the front door. She said she had guessed I would be at your party. I had been coaxing her to take me. She found me, somehow, in the dark and said she wanted to tell me something. Well, there was plenty I wanted to tell *her* and so we went out into the front hall where nobody could hear us. Then the door opened, just the way you said it did in the Burlingame house. I was so scared! I'm not sure what happened after that. Maybe I fainted but I'm sure I must have screamed first. I thought it was the ghost. But in the morning, somehow, I was back at the Vincent's again."

"And we hunted for you nearly all night."

"You poor things! You must have thought terrible things about me, promising to tell who I was and everything and then just disappearing—like that.'' She snapped her fingers expressively. ''Didn't you think I did it on purpose?''

''Well, maybe, just at first,'' Judy confessed, ''but then Marge said Kay had been there and I found your handkerchief with an initial V on it. You had asked so many questions about the will. I guessed the rest.''

''I was going to tell you. I just wanted to make sure you and Peter were on my side. I intended to look at the will and, then if he would, I wanted Peter to be my special guardian.''

''Do you hear that?'' cried Judy. ''That's why Sally wanted to go to the courthouse with us! It is our case after all!''

Peter, in the driver's seat, nodded.

''I guessed as much,'' he said. But his brief words could not conceal the pleasure in his voice.

CHAPTER XX

"WHERE are we going?" asked Sally presently. They had passed Peter's law office in Roulsville without stopping and were now driving straight across the town.

Judy hesitated. The original plan had been to stop and see if they could find Dr. Burlingame somewhere in his closed and mysterious house. But now that they had Sally and everything seemed so safe and right again, she was not too enthusiastic about throwing her into a new danger. How did she know Dr. Burlingame had taken Sally back to the Vincents? The girl had been frightened in his house and he might be in league with Harry Vincent. Oh, she hoped not! That would spoil Sally's chances of ever recovering her property since he was the only living witness to her uncle's will.

"Suppose we buy some milk at a grocery store and get ready for that picnic before we decide where we're going," she suggested.

189

Everybody approved of this idea most heartily. At the next corner they stopped and Horace went into a store and bought a quart of milk, some paper cups and a large container filled with creamy potato salad. For dessert, he suggested that they pick their own wild strawberries.

"I know where we can find some luscious ones," said Judy. "There's a field right near Dr. Burlingame's house. What do you suppose would happen if we had our picnic lunch there?"

"He might come out and chase us—" Horace began.

"And suppose he does! We'd see him, wouldn't we? And that's what we want."

Sally looked at her curiously. "He's the man who's supposed to live in that house where you found me, isn't he?" she asked. "Why do you want to see him? And why do you think he'd chase us out of his field when he just kept quiet and let us cook our dinner and wander all over his house?"

"I don't know," Judy admitted. "How would you go about seeing a man like that?"

"I wouldn't," she said. "I wouldn't want to see him. It was bad enough just hearing his voice."

"You never told us that," said Judy in surprise.

"I saw and heard so much. I didn't want you to think I was quite crazy. But I did hear a voice say, 'Stay as long as you like. Search the house if you want to . . .' and I was too frightened to listen any more and covered my head. It was like Beauty and the Beast. The beast spoke that way to Beauty *and he was just a voice*. I know exactly how she felt."

"But that was a fairy story."

"So is this," laughed Sally, never serious for long. "I'm still a princess in disguise. They wouldn't let me wear the dress you gave me."

"You'll be wearing your own dresses," Judy told her, "when we win our case."

She had not yet mentioned the note in her pocketbook signed "Uncle Lou." There were a great many things she had not yet mentioned— things that puzzled her and which Sally could probably explain if she only would. But it would be better, she decided, to bring out her story gradually. They could talk while they were having lunch.

It was a beautiful day. Everything was green and glistening after the storm. Here and there along the road they could see where the wind had uprooted trees or broken them off at the top. The cement still bore traces of the muddy water that had covered it. Streams were still high, but all morning the sun had been shining. It went under a cloud just as they turned down the road that had been used as a detour two days before. It soon reappeared but when they came in sight of Dr. Burlingame's house the cloud still hovered above it. Sally shivered and pointed.

"You see! It's such a gloomy place that the sun won't even shine on it. No wonder it's full of ghosts."

"I hope the ghosts won't wait until midnight to appear," remarked Peter as he stopped the car right near the doctor's mail box. The field across the road from the gloomy house looked like a splendid picnic place. There was a stream running through it and, beside the stream, were rocks and clumps of shady trees.

"It looks okay to me," said Horace, beginning to unload various parcels from the back of the car. Soon, with everybody carrying something, they started walking along the road. Sally lingered only a little way behind.

"Couldn't we fix the lunch on one of these rocks?" she called presently.

They turned.   The rock she had indicated was large and flat—an ideal table.   It was shaded by the bushes that grew around it, making it a fairly secluded place.

"I guess it isn't too far away," Peter observed.   "We can still keep an eye on Dr. Burlingame's house and, if the doctor happens to step out, one of us can run over and speak to him."

"You're elected," laughed Judy.   "You're the lawyer.   But I'll go with you.   I wouldn't miss it for the world."

"I'll stay right here if you don't mind," Sally announced, perching herself on a jutting ledge where she continued to sit, swinging her feet and kicking against the rock.

Judy handed her a corn muffin and then began dishing potato salad from the container into the paper cups Horace had bought.

"There aren't any forks," she observed sadly.

"That," said Horace, "was a deliberate scheme.   Now we shall have to go up to the old gentleman's house and borrow some."

"Oh, please!" begged Sally, her blue eyes pleading.   "Don't spoil things now.   Let's each lunch first and then go up if we have to.   You have a jackknife, haven't you? You can whittle out sticks for forks.''

The sticks worked splendidly. Horace found it easier to spear the pieces of potato while he kept one eye on the house. Judy and Peter worked them something like chop sticks, laughing and talking and trying to show the trick to Sally. The girl needed some nourishment before they began questioning her. But finally Judy, unable to restrain her curiosity, ventured, ''If Dr. Burlingame's house frightens you so, Sally, how did you happen to be there all alone when we found you?''

''Oh, I can tell you that,'' laughed Sally unexpectedly. ''That was just a mistake. I thought that was your house and so I prowled around in it hunting for the secret cellar. I'm sorry if I frightened you with that lamp——''

''That was the lamp you had been using then —that oil lamp we found down cellar? And then you blew it out and came upstairs and hid in the dark?''

She nodded. ''I'd been there quite a while. It was when I first began hunting that the voice yelled at me. 'Search the house if you want to.' But, of course, I didn't search any more after you came. I knew I wouldn't have found anything if I had.''

''But you did find something in our house?'' Judy prompted her.

''Nothing but that empty box. You saw me trying to hide it. But I wasn't taking anything that didn't belong to me. I was supposed to use whatever was in the box—or I thought I was,'' she added, her face clouding. ''I never told anybody about it because it was our secret.''

''Yours and your uncle Lou's?''

Sally gasped and her face went white.

''How—how did you know?''

''I found this,'' said Judy and placed the note in her hand.

All three of them watched her as she read it. A bird was singing in a tree not far from the rock but, for a while, there was no other sound. Then Sally looked up.

''I'm so glad he took it,'' she said. ''I thought maybe somebody had stolen it. But if he took it—why, that makes everything all right. He put it there in case of emergency.''

''But what was it, Sally? What was supposed to be in the box?''

''I'm not sure,'' she replied, speaking slowly,

"but I think there must have been some money. There may have been something else too. I don't remember. I was only eight years old when he told me about it. He said it would be mine some day and I should save it, just as he always had, for an emergency. He believed in being prepared in case something should happen —and then it did." She paused for a moment, apparently lost in thought. "He lived with us before the accident, you know."

"In that house where Kay's family live now?" Horace questioned.

She nodded. "He was on his way home when the accident happened. I'll never forget it. We had the table fixed so beautifully to surprise him. We waited and waited. And then a policeman came and told us he'd gone over the bank and into the river. My mother died a little while after that—and then Dad. And then when Uncle Harry's family moved in and took all their things—well, that was just too much. I thought that was an emergency and if I could get hold of the emergency box I could use the money in it and run away. Uncle Lou had told me how to find it."

"Seven times seven. Was that it?" asked Judy. "I found the note in your pocket. I guess you didn't know those same directions were also on the will. Someone had tried to erase them."

"That's queer," she said. "But maybe Uncle Lou did it himself after he took what was in the box. I didn't see the note he had left. Where was it?"

"It fluttered out somehow when we moved the stone. We found Blackberry playing with it. Sally, what do you suppose the emergency was?"

"I don't know," she answered thoughtfully. "It might have been his burns. I never saw him after the explosion. The doctor wouldn't let anybody see him."

"The doctor!" exclaimed Peter who, all this time had been perched beside her listening. "Sally, did you know that doctor was also a witness to your uncle's will? And did you know that his name was Burlingame?"

"Dr. Burlingame isn't a real doctor," said Sally positively. "He's a ghost."

"Sally dear," said Judy, getting up from her seat on the rock and collecting what was left of the lunch things, "if you could see him and talk with him, you'd believe he was real, wouldn't you? I don't pretend to understand these ghosts of yours but I saw one too and I know how you feel. The difference is, *I believe they can all be explained.*"

"You can't explain it," said Sally, "when you see someone you know is dead."

"Perhaps that someone is still alive and looking for you, Sally."

"Oh, no!" she cried. "He'd see me then. He wouldn't just appear and—and haunt me and then go away. But let's not talk about it any more. I told you that you can't explain ghosts."

"We can't," Judy agreed, "but perhaps Dr. Burlingame can. Come on, everybody, we've put it off long enough! Some time before this trial we've got to see him."

CHAPTER XXI

RELUCTANTLY, Sally slid down from her perch and they started off—all four of them—in the direction of the house. In their sudden enthusiasm, they had forgotten to collect all their picnic things. The milk bottle, the four empty containers and the box that had held the fig newtons were still spread out on top of the rock.

The house looked as bleak and deserted as ever but, as they approached it, Peter pointed out a little row of buildings behind it. They were small and nobody had paid any attention to them before.

"He keeps chickens!" joked Horace. "Ghosts don't keep chickens, Sally. He must come out of the house sometimes to feed them. But perhaps he doesn't give them anything in the middle of the day."

"I think I'd like to try the back door this time," Judy announced. "Maybe he's more hospitable to people who come to the back door."

There was a well worn path around to the back porch. As they passed the windows something seemed to be moving about behind the blinds but, as all of them were tightly drawn, it was hard to tell whether or not anybody was really there. A series of curious squeaks greeted them as they came nearer to the little houses.

"Chickens don't squeak——" Horace began.

"But white mice and guinea pigs do! Look!" cried Judy, running over to the little houses and peering in through the wire screen. "It is! It is! I don't believe he's crazy at all. He just wants to be alone to do his work. It must be important if he keeps white mice and guinea pigs for his experiments."

"Oh!" gasped Sally. "That must have been what squeaked."

"Don't tell me these were all the ghosts you saw——"

"Oh, no! I didn't see these before. I just heard them. What sort of experiments do you think he makes—not—not calling back spirits. That would be so cruel."

"No," said Judy decidedly. "He wouldn't call back spirits with guinea pigs. What makes you say that?"

"Because I saw the—the ghost here.   He rapped on the door and I looked out and there he was—just as though he were alive.   He didn't ring the bell.   He just rapped with his cane and then a voice shouted, 'Go away!' and he went."

"How did he go?   Just walk away?"

"I don't know," she cried.   "There were two or three ghosts then.   I began to feel dizzy and then I knew I was seeing things."

"Poor Sally!   I don't wonder, but this first ghost," questioned Judy, "was he—did he look anything like your uncle Lou?"

"A little," she admitted.   "But he wasn't the same.   I don't want to stay around this place.   It is haunted whether people know it or not and I couldn't bear it to see him looking at me like that again."

"It may have been Dr. Burlingame himself," Horace spoke up more loudly.   "Everybody knows he is a little queer."

"Could it have been Dr. Burlingame?"

"I don't know," Sally said.   "I never saw him."

"You will in a minute," Peter prophesied. "What's that?"

There was the noise of something creaking inside the house, then a scraping sound as of a chair being pushed toward the wall, followed by a terrific banging and thumping on the inside of the back windows.

"Go away!" a voice suddenly thundered.

Sally turned to run but Judy held her.

"It's the doctor!" she exclaimed. "Don't you dare run away just when we've finally made him notice us. If we keep on standing here eventually he'll have to come out——"

Thump! Thump! The banging sounded louder on the window.

Sally was shaking like a leaf.

"You're safe with us, dear," Judy spoke more gently. "Nothing can happen to you while you're with us——"

"Go away!" the voice thundered again. "I don't see people. Go away!"

"We'd better go. He can't come out!" cried Sally, still trembling. "He's only a voice. A voice is all that lives there."

"A voice can't hurt us—" Peter began.

But he was interrupted by a final explosion of words from inside the shuttered house.

"Get out of here and be quick about it or I'll have the law on you for trespassing! I've told Harry Vincent and I'll tell him again. I won't have any more people snooping around my property. I'll be at the trial. I've already told him that. But Lou Vincent was my friend and when I get on the witness stand I intend to tell the truth and nothing but the truth. I won't be advised by anybody's lawyer."

"Good for you!" shouted Peter. "That's the way to talk. The truth is all we want. Now tell us, who else has been snooping around your property?"

"I'm telling you nothing—absolutely nothing —you nor Harry Vincent nor any of the rest of his crooked lawyers."

"It might interest you to know that I'm not Harry Vincent's lawyer. I'm working on the other side of the case, for Ned Vincent's little girl, Sally. This is Sally with us now——"

The door was suddenly opened. As one, the four young people stepped back, speechless with surprise, as Dr. Burlingame stepped out. He was real. There was no doubt of that, but the poor man did look as though he needed someone to iron his shirts and fix his ties. It must have been a long time since he had had a hair cut. Judy looked long and hard at him. But, definitely, he was not her midnight visitor. He wore thick glasses but, behind them, his eyes crinkled as he turned to Sally.

"So this is Ned Vincent's little girl? It's about time you came to see your father's old friend. What have they been doing to you, child? You're as thin as a rail and as white as chalk. But you're here for no good reason," he continued, turning to Peter. "I've heard about you and your secretary. Think you're a couple of detectives, don't you? Well, I won't have people finding out things for Harry Vincent and you're his lawyer's assistant. He said so."

Peter's face turned quite red.

"He was taking a lot for granted. He asked me but I—I didn't take the case."

He had been about to say, "I refused." Judy could tell that. Oh, how she wished he had been able to refuse.

"I told you Uncle Harry was here," said Sally, her eyes still fastened on the doctor as though, any minute, he might disappear. "It was the other time I hid in the car. He came in to look for something and I followed him. I—I guess I scared him a little hiding under the furniture covers——"

Dr. Burlingame interrupted with a laugh that was more like a roar.

"Ha! Ha! Ha!" he roared. "So you were the little ghost that frightened away your prying old uncle. And Kay and Dickie—*ha! ha! ha!* I can still see those youngsters running. The Lord only knows what they would have taken if it hadn't been for you. By the way, young lady," he added, "perhaps you didn't know this furniture that's stored here once belonged to your uncle Lou. Thought I was queer, didn't you, keeping it all covered up like that? Well, some day when you have a home of your own you'll be glad enough I took care of it."

"Oh, thank you! Thank you!" she cried. "I thought it looked as though I'd seen it."

"Another time I'll ask you in," he promised, "but a bachelor's quarters need to be made presentable."

"Another time," announced Sally, now her laughing self again, "we'll ring the bell seven short rings. That will be our signal and you'll know then that we haven't come for anything on earth but to see you and have a visit."

"I'll know," he said. "A lonely old man should be glad enough of young company."

Peter stood trying to figure things out as the others talked with the surprising and somewhat pathetic old doctor. He seemed delighted when Judy promised to bring her father to see him.

"Renewing old friendships," he chuckled.

"Maybe that's what I need. Harry Vincent had me hating the sight of my fellow men. I could have had the law on him for breaking the lock and entering my house without permission, but it was simpler to ignore him and let the truth come up at the trial. My white mice and guinea pigs here are better company."

"Are they doing good work for you, doctor?" Horace asked. Dr. Burlingame's work had aroused his curiosity. There might be a story in it.

"Teaching me something about the nervous system," he replied shortly. "There's a lot to learn."

"My father said you were an eye, ear, nose and throat specialist," Judy put in. "Perhaps you could tell me. Do the nerves have anything to do with—with what people see?"

"Just what are you getting at?" he questioned. She could see he was beginning to be impatient as well as still a trifle suspicious.

"The truth is," she confessed, "we're very, very much interested in your house because Sally tells us you had another visitor. It may have been Lou Vincent himself."

"What sort of nonsense is this?" snorted the

doctor, looking suddenly fierce again. "Lou Vincent is dead."

"That was what we thought until several people began thinking they had seen his ghost."

"Maybe they did," said the doctor gruffly. "There are several people he ought to haunt. And now, young lady, no matter which side of the case you and your friends are on, I'm bidding you good day. I suppose I shall see you all again at the court house."

"Good day, Dr. Burlingame. We'll be there all right," Peter said.

And then the door closed.

"Well, we didn't find out much about Lou Vincent," said Judy when they were all back in the car again and ready to start for home.

"Who cares?" said Peter. "Dr. Burlingame's on our side and that was all I wanted to know. Harry Vincent's been pestering him. That's why he wouldn't see people. But Sally fixed that. Now let's hurry home before she changes her mind about her special guardian."

"After this visit," she said with happy satisfaction, "I wouldn't change it for the world."

CHAPTER XXII

Court opened officially at ten o'clock on the day the will was to be contested. But long before that time Judy and her friends were down at the courthouse. They lingered a few moments on the lawn, still talking over the many possibilities of the case. Sally was worried.

"If Dr. Burlingame doesn't come," she said, "we won't have a single witness to say Uncle Lou wrote the will—and I know he did."

"I know it too. Don't worry, Sally," Judy tried to cheer her. "Peter and Mr. Pierce are both sure he'll be here."

Mr. Pierce was the lawyer appointed by the court to defend the will. All week Judy and Peter had been busy collecting evidence and planning the case with him.

Sally had not returned to Harry Vincent's after she had signed the petition and Peter had become her special guardian. Her explanations had been so confused that it had been impossible to learn just what she had seen or where, and

Peter actually feared for her safety at her uncle's place. So it had been arranged for her to stay in the guest room at Judy's home—the same guest room that had been Honey's and Scottie's when Judy had been trying to solve other mysteries.

Some time had been spent in the office each day, but as very little business came in, Judy's afternoons had been free to help Peter scout around. The furniture factory had yielded a number of papers in Lou Vincent's handwriting. But the note they had found in the cellar and the signature on the will were a little different from the factory samples. That probably proved something but Judy couldn't imagine what. Eager for the trial to begin, she and Sally went up as soon as the courtroom was open.

Although Judy felt that it was her case almost as much as it was Peter's, she could not sit at the counsel table with him. Sally might have been allowed that honor but, at the last moment, she was struck with something very close to stage fright. She would be facing her uncle's family and they would be trying to prove that her father had committed a crime—that of forging a will. She dreaded the ordeal.

"What if they win the case?" she asked in an awed whisper as she and Judy entered the almost empty courtroom. Its high ceiling and massive oak panels made them both feel very small.

"We have to keep them from winning," Judy told her. "Sally, you must not get panicky in the witness chair. Just tell the truth. That's all Peter wants any of his witnesses to do."

She would speak of Peter as the only lawyer to oppose Mr. Sanders. Actually there were three—the venerable and kindly Mr. Pierce, his son and assistant who was a boy not much older than Peter and only lately admitted to the bar, and Peter himself. He sat with the other two at a long table just in front of the rail which enclosed the judge's seat, the witness chair and the desk where the court stenographer sat. This table was called the counsel table and on one side of it sat the lawyers who were in favor of the will as it had been written. On the other side were the lawyers hired by Harry Vincent to contest the will. Mr. Sanders headed this group. Then came the assistant who had taken Peter's place and two special guardians for Kay and Dickie Vincent.

"As if they needed guardians!" sniffed Sally

when Judy pointed them out. "Trust Uncle Harry to see that the rights of his own children are protected."

"But you're his own niece——"

"That's different," said Sally.

She stood clutching Judy's arm and gazing about the courtroom. She still found it hard to believe that there could be a trial without a jury.

"It doesn't seem fair," she continued after they had taken their seats in the front row where they could see everything clearly. "The judge shouldn't be allowed to decide everything alone. It's like having a king instead of a president."

The judge's seat with its deep red cushion and high, carved back did look a little like a throne. He was not yet seated at his high desk inside the rail. But the court stenographer was there all ready to take her notes. Horace, too, was taking notes for the newspaper. He came in quietly and sat down just the other side of Sally. Several of Judy's friends came in with him, among them Scottie, Selma and Peter's sister Honey who wouldn't have missed the trial for anything. Lois, Lorraine and Arthur entered just as the judge took his seat.

The judge was white haired and dignified.

Sitting in the carved chair at his desk under the lamp glow he seemed to typify justice. Behind him were hangings of red velvet to match the chair cushions and draperies at the windows. Just above the hangings was a copy of scales, equally balanced, engraved in the oak panel. Underneath were the printed words:

"Justice, when equal scales she holds, is blind;
  Nor cruelty, nor mercy, change her mind."

"Those scales are supposed to be held in the hand of blind justice," Judy whispered, glancing up at them. "They show us the way the judge is supposed to hear the evidence and weigh it in his mind. I hope he does."

"I hope so too," agreed Sally, settling back in her chair with a sigh.

The courtroom was rapidly filling up. The Vincent family came in looking as though they were quite accustomed to trials. Kay held her head high, well aware of the fact that the little hat she was wearing made her appear younger and more innocent than she really was. She smiled sweetly at Sally as she passed her but her cousin, not so practiced in the art of deception, returned her smile with a scowl that was unmistakably fierce.

"The meanie!" she whispered to Judy. "I wish I hadn't worn the new clothes she sent me."

Judy was still wondering why the Vincents had been so generous about sending Sally's clothes as soon as they learned that she was staying at the Bolton's and why, of all times, they had chosen to include a brand new outfit. It looked newer and more stylish than Kay's. Why, that was the reason! Judy decided, too late, that Sally was right. She shouldn't have worn the new clothes.

Among the first of the witnesses was the handwriting expert that Mr. Sanders had called in. He had studied the various samples of handwriting that Judy and Peter and others working on the case had collected and compared them with the handwriting on the will.

"And what are your findings?" asked Mr. Pierce, questioning for Sally's side of the case.

"I find there are slight discrepancies. The handwriting is similar but not exactly the same. Now, your honor, may I introduce this note in evidence?"

He handed the judge the note Judy had found in the cellar but, before he would admit it, Judy herself was called to the witness stand and que)-

tioned by Mr. Sanders. She told, as simply as she could, the story of their search in the cellar. Even to her own ears it sounded fantastic.

"You say your attention was drawn to this note that had fallen to the floor?" Mr. Sanders questioned with his best sarcasm. "How was it drawn? Who pointed it out?"

"My cat," said Judy. "He was playing with it."

Almost everybody in the courtroom laughed. Even the judge, usually so solemn, smiled a little.

"Your honor," cried Mr. Sanders. "I object to this note being admitted in evidence. It was found under peculiar circumstances, to say the least, and we have no actual proof that Lou Vincent ever wrote it."

"Objection sustained," said the judge.

Judy walked back to her seat beside Sally in a daze, hardly able to realize that her most important clue had been thrown out of the case.

"Does he mean the handwriting expert can't say what he thinks about the note?" asked Sally.

Judy nodded. "There was no proof that your uncle Lou wrote it."

"But he did—" Then Sally herself stopped. It was true. There was no proof. The hand-

writing was more like that on the will than anything else they had found. But it could not be
admitted.

The handwriting expert now began comparing the signature on the will with the handwriting on one of Ned Vincent's bank cards. Judy
and Sally held fast to each other's hands. On
the other side of them Horace had his pencil
poised, ready to write. Peter was sitting, white-
faced, at the counsel table. The same thought
was in all their minds. He mustn't point out
any similarity.

"This peculiar loop on the *t* is common to
both hands. Both *v's* begin with a small loop.
Both signatures have a similar slant."

"Would you say they were written by the
same hand?" asked Mr. Sanders.

"They might have been. But again," testified the handwriting expert, "they might have
been written by two people who had worked together and studied together. Two brothers
often have handwritings as similar as these."

"May I frame my question again, your
honor?" Mr. Sanders asked politely.

With the judge's permission, he turned again
to the witness and asked, "Would you say with
reasonable certainty that the two signatures

might have been written by the same hand?"

"I said there is a strong resemblance."

"By a strong resemblance do you mean that the two hands are alike?"

"Something alike."

The handwriting expert was beginning to fidget in the witness chair but Mr. Sanders continued. "Could you say with reasonable certainty that they are alike?"

At that Peter whispered something to Mr. Pierce on his side of the counsel table and the older lawyer got excitedly to his feet.

"I object, your honor. The opposing counsel is putting words in the mouth of the witness."

"Objection overruled," said the judge turning to Mr. Sanders. "You may proceed."

"I repeat the question. Could you say with reasonable certainty that the two hands are alike?"

"I could," replied the handwriting expert.

Judy could hardly keep her seat. Mr. Sanders was making this witness testify exactly the way he wanted him to. Now it was Mr. Pierce's turn. How she wished Peter could ask the questions himself instead of just sitting there whispering suggestions. A trial was supposed to be fair but this wasn't. Mr. Pierce began

questioning the supposed expert about his quali-
fications and experience. He was vague at first
but quite willing to mention other cases—some
famous ones—in which he had been called in to
testify as a handwriting expert. Mr. Pierce
tried to show the court that he had been in-
fluenced to testify in Mr. Sanders' favor since
he was the lawyer who had called him in. The
judge, however, did not seem very much impressed.

"We're losing the case," wailed Sally, almost
aloud. "They can't prove my father forged
a will when he didn't."

But Judy knew a clever lawyer crook could
and very often did prove things that were quite
the opposite of the truth. Witness after witness
testified against the will. The hidden writing,
with which they had hoped to prove so much,
seemed of little importance since seven times
seven merely marked a hiding place and the
will stood as it was first written.

Sally was called to the stand and, to Judy's
great disappointment, made a bad impression.
Mr. Sanders pointed out the clothes she was
wearing as proof that her guardian, Harry
Vincent, had been good to her.

"He bought me these on purpose to show me

off," Sally declared, looking daggers at her uncle's family. "They were so mean to me that I almost wanted to die."

"They let you keep your little dog, Woofer, didn't they?" asked Mr. Sanders. "I understand he was quite a nuisance. But they allowed you to keep this troublesome pet because your father had given him to you. I wouldn't call that being mean, would you?"

"I don't know what it was," cried Sally, bursting into tears. "But they were m-mean to W-woofer."

Kay was then questioned about the dog and about various other matters and denied everything Sally had said. Finally the all important question of whether or not Lou Vincent was able to write a will came up for argument. Judy almost held her breath. Now they would call Dr. Burlingame and he would tell the truth. She had seen him come in, a little late, and was pinning her hopes on what he would say. To her this was the big moment in the trial. If he had actually seen Lou Vincent write and sign the will then Sally would surely be allowed to inherit her uncle's property.

CHAPTER XXIII

THE TRUTH AT LAST

His name was called and a stir was heard in the court room as he stood up. Even in his worn suit and badly ironed shirt Dr. Burlingame was an impressive figure. Judy turned all the way around in her seat to see him, following him with her eyes as he walked to the witness chair.

"Do you swear before the ever-living God to tell the truth, the whole truth and nothing but the truth?" the judge asked, very fast in his usual manner.

The doctor's answer was not hurried. With his right hand raised solemnly, he thundered so that his voice could be heard over the entire court room, "I do!"

Mr. Pierce was first to question him. Standing next to the rail and leaning expectantly forward, he asked him to testify as to whether or not Lou Vincent wrote the will and signed it in his presence.

"He did," declared the doctor. "He wrote it on my typewriter and signed it with my fountain pen. My wife and I then signed our names as witnesses."

"Thank you," said the lawyer with satisfaction. "That is all."

Peter whispered something but he shook his head. The truth ought to speak for itself. But Mr. Pierce had hardly seated himself at the head of his side of the counsel table when Mr. Sanders, on the other side, leaped to his feet and began firing questions over the rail. How badly was Lou Vincent burned? Did he have the use of his hands? Was he able to typewrite and sign a will?

"He was," said the doctor quite calmly. "I saw him do it."

"Why did you keep him at your house instead of returning him to his home after the accident? Wasn't it because he was unable to return home?" Mr. Sanders demanded.

"It was not," he replied, "I kept him there because I wished to treat his eyes."

"You haven't told us anything about his eyes, doctor," said Mr. Sanders with a smirk. "Just what was the matter with his eyes?"

"There was plenty the matter," replied the

doctor vehemently. "His brother Harry, the same brother who is now contesting his will, had ordered a new kind of furniture polish for the men to use at the furniture factory. He neglected to tell anybody that it was highly explosive and when Lou Vincent opened the can it blew up in his face."

"The furniture polish blew up and yet you're trying to tell me that his hands were not injured?"

"They were not. He could use them as well as I can use my own hands, better perhaps. There wasn't a burn on them."

"Then why were you treating him? If he was not burned why was it necessary to keep him at your home for treatment?"

The doctor scowled fiercely.

"I told you. I was treating his eyes. I had hoped to save his sight."

The smile on Mr. Sanders' face widened. He had scored a point.

"We have a witness here who expects to testify that he was temporarily blinded," he said. "Is this true?"

"No," roared Dr. Burlingame. "He was permanently blinded. That was the result and the only result of the explosion. But he didn't need to see to typewrite. I showed him where the line was and if his signature is a little shaky that's the reason. He couldn't see——"

"Just a minute. Did you typewrite this will or did this blind man?"

"He did!"

Mr. Sanders smiled at the judge as much as to say, "The poor man doesn't know what he is saying," and then he began asking unmerciful questions about his dead wife and the daughter who had run away and his commitment to a hospital for the insane. It was temporary loss of memory because of grief, Dr. Burlingame insisted. In spite of objections from Mr. Pierce and silent fury from Peter and the young assistant, the questioning was allowed to go on.

Finally Dr. Burlingame was forced to admit that he himself had erased the "seven times seven" on the will for fear Harry Vincent would find the emergency box and Sally would be cheated out of everything.

Mr. Sanders was unmerciful, gaining point after point, and when they were through with the poor doctor he fairly stumbled out of the witness chair and out of the courtroom. Judy looked up at the scales above the judge's head—the scales that were supposed to stand for justice.

"It's a wonder they don't fall on somebody," she said.

Sally turned to her, those clear blue eyes of hers bleak with distress.

"He was blind!" she said. "Uncle Lou was blind!"

Through a fog they heard the judge's voice, "Court adjourned." There would be another day of it. Judy had already guessed what would happen—more witnesses to testify in favor of the Vincents and finally the case decided in their favor. Peter looked white, beaten.

"What's a fellow to do," he said, joining them at the massive door, "when you can't believe people under oath?"

"I believe Dr. Burlingame," said Judy. "Lou Vincent was my midnight visitor and all this is useless if we can only find him. Sally, do you realize why he frightened you so? He couldn't see you. Somehow, he escaped from that wrecked car and all this time he's been wandering around—blind. Nobody knew he had been blinded but Dr. Burlingame. He must have promised not to tell in the hope that he could save his sight. Then, when he had failed, Lou Vincent and this other young man—what was his name?"

"Ray Suffern," Sally supplied quickly. "I saw him too. That was what I meant—and there was a woman all in white. When you see one person you know is dead you begin to get scared and then, when you see two——"

"You saw Ray Suffern!" Judy interrupted, her eyes flashing. "Then neither of them was killed. I'm beginning to see it all—the accident and everything. Now I think I know exactly what must have happened. They jumped from the car. They could have, you know, with Ray Suffern to help. Then he and Lou Vincent went back and helped themselves to the contents of the emergency box. That was what he meant in his note and that's why the writing was shaky, the same as it was on the will. The emergency was the fact that he was blind. He must have known everybody would think he had been killed when the wrecked car was found. He *wanted* them to think that. And he didn't want them to know he was blind. I don't believe Dr. Burlingame ever would have told if he hadn't taken the oath. But what a strange secret! There's more to the story, of course, but can't you see it too? We'll lose this case but that doesn't matter now. The only way to win it is to lose it and then find Lou Vincent. I don't know about such things but tell me, Peter, what does happen when a man who has been declared legally dead returns?"

"The law says he may sue for the recovery of his property," Peter declared, "and I'd be glad to help him."

"You'd be his lawyer, wouldn't you?" cried Sally. "You'd be the one to ask the questions. But what would you be trying to prove?"

"Nothing," said Peter, "except that your uncle Lou is the person he claims to be and that ought to be easy—if he returns."

"But will he?" wailed Sally. "Just think, if I hadn't been so foolish he'd be here now. If I'd only have asked, 'Is that you, Uncle Lou?' when he stood looking at me and not seeing me! And Dr. Burlingame thought he was Uncle Harry come back to pester him with more questions and so he shouted for him to go away. I guess Uncle Lou must have thought nobody wanted him any more."

"Not a very warm welcome for anyone practically returned from the dead," Peter agreed. "I can understand his disappointment."

"He was disappointed. I guess that's why he didn't answer when I tried to call him in out of the storm. He had just been turned away by Dr. Burlingame and then, when he came back to his old home, a second rebuff was about all he needed to leave him practically in a daze. It was my fault too,'' Judy went on. ''If I hadn't been so frightened by the way he looked at me I would have asked him in out of the storm before that tree fell and kept us from seeing what happened to him. Now we've got to find out. You can help us, Horace,'' she added, turning to her brother who had been too busy trying to get everything straight in his mind to say a word. ''Please, just this once, let's write up this story together. It ought to be the biggest scoop your paper has had in years.''

CHAPTER XXIV

WHEN THE STORY WAS PRINTED

THE story, when it appeared the following morning, told everybody in bold headlines:

**Lou Vincent, Missing for
Seven Years, Declared Legally Dead
Brother Contests His Will in Court This Week
Niece Who Inherits Property under the
Will Claims Her Uncle Still Lives
Pleads for His Return**

Under these headlines, in smaller type, the whole story of Judy's midnight visitor was told. It was connected with Horace's other story which he had headed GIRL SEES GHOST, only now the ghost was identified as Lou Vincent and the girl as Sally. Nothing was left out. Sally's picture was beside the article. The photograph was not a recent one, but a picture she had had taken seven years before. In it she was standing beside her uncle Lou who was sitting in a chair and who bore only a faint resemblance to the older, sadder Lou Vincent who had returned —blind—only to find himself a stranger.

Even though Lou Vincent himself would not be able to read the story or recognize the picture there was a chance that Ray Suffern, the man who must have been his friend and helper during his seven years' absence, could describe it and read the article aloud. It had been copied by several city papers.

"Mr. Lee says it's taking a big chance," Horace said as he showed off the paper at the breakfast table.

Mr. Lee was the editor and, if Judy and her brother hadn't been of great service to the paper before, she knew he would not have risked the story.

"Harry Vincent can sue us if we're wrong, can't he?" she asked.

Horace nodded, biting thoughtfully into a doughnut.

"Then we'll have to be right. But what a stir there will be in the Vincent family this morning!" She smiled at Sally, eating her breakfast beside her. "I can hardly wait to see your uncle Harry's face."

"Do I have to go to court with you?" she

asked. "He'll be so mad and, really, the whole story is based on what I said and he'll try and make me deny it."

"It's going to look bad for him if he creates a scene in the courtroom," Judy began, but Sally interrupted quickly with a willing, "I'll go." But the trial was unimportant to her now. She didn't want her uncle Lou's property if it were possible to have him instead.

Harry Vincent, clever crook that he was, created no scene. In fact, he did not so much as mention the newspaper article when he met Judy and Sally in court an hour or so later. The trial proceeded with the usual dignity of trials as more witnesses were called to testify against the will. The thing that they were dwelling upon now was the fact that Lou Vincent or "the blind man" as Mr. Sanders now called him, was unable to typewrite. Several people who had known him quite well stated that they had never seen him use a typewriter. He would have needed to know the touch system to have been able to typewrite after he had become blind.

Judy herself could typewrite with her eyes closed. A great many people could. It seemed so reasonable to her and yet Mr. Sanders made it sound so impossible. What a surprise it would be for him as well as for Harry Vincent if, just when they thought they were winning the case, Lou Vincent should walk into the courtroom. Judy sat on the edge of her chair, almost expecting such a thing to happen, but the case went on to its finish and was decided, as she had known it would be, in Harry Vincent's favor. Sally would now receive only a portion of her uncle's property. The court ruled that it should be decided exactly as it would have been if there had been no will.

"And now," asked Sally, "what am I to do?"

"Just wait," Judy told her hopefully. "You still have a room at our house. Something may happen yet."

But Judy had never been a very patient person herself. Waiting was one of the hardest things she did and so, the day after the trial, she decided it might be wise to call on Dr. Burlingame and find out what he thought of the story that had been in the paper. Her theory of the accident had been set forth in print but would Dr. Burlingame think it possible? He had stated so emphatically, "Lou Vincent is dead." Why had he said that, she wondered. How much of the story had Dr. Burlingame told the court and how much of it was still a secret? Determined to leave no stone unturned in her efforts to locate Lou Vincent, Judy approached her father and begged him to go with her.

"I told him you'd call, Dad," she said, "and he'll be expecting you."

Finally Dr. Bolton consented. It was Sunday and so he had no regular office hours. He, too, was eager to renew the old friendship with Dr. Burlingame.

"May I go too?" asked Sally. "He'll let me in. You remember the secret signal I told him about—seven short rings? Uncle Lou and I used to have such a signal."

"I'm the one he doesn't like," said Horace. "This time I'll stay home and let Judy bring me the news if there is any."

"If there is any," Judy promised, "I'll bring it. I'm still curious to find out who opened that door."

But her thoughts were troubled as they started off in her father's car. Suppose Dr. Burlingame had proof that Lou Vincent was dead! Suppose her midnight visitor was only some impostor hired by Harry Vincent to frighten her! She realized that she and Horace should have talked with Dr. Burlingame before the newspaper ever printed that story. Harry Vincent could sue the editor if she had guessed wrong.

"Why do I get into such mixups?" she complained, moving closer to her father. "Most girls aren't always getting involved in other people's troubles. Why am I?"

"Most girls," said Dr. Bolton, smiling at her proudly, "are too much interested in their own problems to see things as clearly as you do. I told you once, Judy girl, that you had a talent for solving mysteries, but it's more than that. It's a talent for straightening out other people's lives for them. Just think of the people who are happier because you've worked out their problems." He began listing them—"Honey, Irene, Scottie, even the editor's daughter, pretty Lorraine Lee——"

"But not Sally," Judy interrupted.

"No," her father said as they turned onto the road that went to Dr. Burlingame's house. "Not yet but very soon. Isn't that the doctor there in the yard now?"

"I guess I won't need my secret signal," said Sally, peering through the windshield. "But what's he doing? Isn't that one of his guinea pigs there on the grass at his feet? Look at him teasing the poor thing! Maybe he is a little queer after all."

As they came closer Dr. Burlingame's behavior seemed stranger still. He had attached a carrot to the end of a string and was pulling it along the grass while the guinea pig followed a little way behind him. He was so much interested in the little animal that he only glanced up as Dr. Bolton stopped the car.

"Dr. Burlingame!" called Judy as she and her father approached with Sally between them. "Remember, I said I'd bring my father and here he is."

"Wait a minute! Don't frighten him," said Dr. Burlingame, holding up his hand and indicating the guinea pig at his feet. "He has it now. He's followed this carrot all the way around my house. What do you think, Dr. Bolton, can he see it or can't he?"

"Of course he can see it," Dr. Bolton replied in a puzzled voice.

"Dr. Burlingame," Sally spoke up quite seriously, "is it true that you're—well, sort of a magician? Can you make things invisible?"

He studied her face a moment before he replied. Then he began to chuckle softly.

"What a notion! How could I make anything invisible? What are you trying to say?"

"She's probably puzzled about the door," Judy put in. "I can't understand it myself. If you're the one who opened it, what ever happened to you afterwards?"

"What happened! You should ask your young lawyer friend that question," he told her fiercely. "When I heard you in my kitchen and got a whiff of those biscuits I thought it was time I came in to see what was up. Naturally I had to be cautious. I tiptoed in from my office where I must have been dozing after Harry Vincent left and opened the door part way, intending to look in. Then something hit me and when I came to there I was slumped down behind the kitchen door with a bump on my head the size of an egg——"

"O-oh!" cried Judy. "What a dreadful thing to have happened. Peter only opened the door quickly to see who was there. He must have banged it back and hit your head and then we never saw you because you were behind it. We could have helped you if we had known."

"But I wasn't talking about the door," Sally objected. "I was talking about the carrot. Why did you think the guinea pig couldn't see it?"

To her surprise, Dr. Burlingame picked up the guinea pig and handed it to her.

"Hold it if you like," he said. "It needs some comforting. It's been through a rather frightening experience. I blinded it——"

"How cruel!" exclaimed Sally, before he could finish.

"Not at all, my dear," replied Dr. Burlingame with a pleased expression. "Do you call it cruelty to make an animal suffer so that human beings can be saved from suffering? Why, this is the climax of seven years' work. If I had known what I know today seven years ago when I operated on your uncle Lou, I might have saved his sight."

"Could you still save it if you could find him?" Judy interrupted eagerly.

"Perhaps," said the doctor. "I saw the newspapers. I can guess why you've come to me, but I'm afraid it's too late. Lou Vincent wanted to die. When I removed the bandages from his eyes and we discovered the operation had failed, he said he'd rather be dead than go on living as a helpless blind man. But I've suspected for a long time that Ray Suffern escaped. That's the only reason I can think of for the disappearance of Alice."

"Alice?" questioned Judy.

"My daughter," Dr. Burlingame explained. "She was fond of the Suffern boy. But so was I. If they had asked me I would have gladly consented to their marriage." He shook his head sadly. "I can't understand it."

"He was here too. I saw him," Sally said. "But you had locked yourself in and I thought they were ghosts. There was a girl too—all in white. Maybe she was Alice."

"Curse me for a fool!" moaned the doctor, sitting down on the porch step and taking his head in his hands.

"I thought your house was Dr. Bolton's," Sally went on. "I was looking for the 'emergency box.'"

"My theory is," Judy put in, "that the emergency box must have provided money for Lou Vincent and Ray Suffern to take a trip to some far away place and start life over again. They might have taken your daughter with them, but it does seem as though she would have written unless there was some quarrel."

"There was no quarrel," Dr. Burlingame said, "none at all. Alice was very dear to both her mother and me. The shock of losing her was too much for her mother." He sighed and lapsed into silence while Dr. Bolton and the two girls stood watching him with sympathy in their hearts. Presently he rose to his feet, took the little guinea pig that Sally had been holding and started toward his pens in back of the house.

"Too late," he murmured. "Too late for this experiment. Too late for anything but failure. I'm a broken old man, Dr. Bolton, but if you can make use of the cure I've discovered, there's still a chance it may help some stranger."

Realizing that it was wise to divert his mind from his troubles, Dr. Bolton allowed the older physician to explain his experiment. The two went inside the house and Judy and Sally followed. Lord Byron was still there, draped in white, as if keeping a ghostly vigil. Under its covers the clock still ticked with loud, calm ticks.

"Your uncle Lou will come back," Judy told Sally hopefully. "He must have meant to come back when he asked Dr. Burlingame to store all his things."

"No," said Sally with a break in her voice. "He meant them—for me. Dr. Burlingame is right. He wanted to die."

"But he didn't die," Judy insisted. "You know he couldn't have because we saw him."

"He's blind," replied Sally hopelessly, "and that's just as bad."

The two girls stood in the hall, fascinated

anew by the strangeness of the doctor's house with its hidden furnishings. Judy's father and Dr. Burlingame were talking near the door that had been locked before. Now it was open and Judy could see beyond it a rather disordered room filled with a doctor's experimental chemicals and test tubes. A cot was along the wall.

Suddenly a bell rang. Judy was too startled' at first to realize that it was only the telephone in the kitchen. She heard Dr. Burlingame's footsteps as he crossed the bare kitchen floor to answer it. Presently he returned and the gray, defeated look had gone out of his face.

"You're wanted at home," he spoke brusquely to Dr. Bolton. "Mind if I come along with you?"

"We'll be delighted," Dr. Bolton assured him.

With no further explanation, the four of them returned to the car. They waited only for Dr. Burlingame to lock his house. The broken lock, Judy saw with relief, had been mended. Now Lou Vincent's furniture was safe. But was he safe? What had happened to make the burly old doctor suddenly so exhuberant?

CHAPTER XXV

THE VISITOR'S RETURN

VERY little was said on the way home. Judy knew something important was about to happen and hardly dared guess what it would be for fear she would be disappointed. Sally's eyes were like stars. There could be only one reason for hurrying home and bringing Dr. Burlingame with them.

"I think I know who's there," she cried, and the moment the car stopped she flew out of it and up the steps.

"Uncle Lou! Uncle Lou!" they heard her excited voice breaking with a happy sob. "How could you ever think you'd be a burden to anybody? Oh, Uncle Lou!"

Judy hurried after her but on the porch she stood dead still, suddenly overwhelmed with what she saw. Lou Vincent, her midnight visitor, and Sally were locked in an embrace that would have broken an ordinary person's ribs. Beside them was a tall youth whom she

239

knew must be Ray Suffern. The third member of this surprising group was a pale girl in a white summer coat. She came forward, stretching out her arms as Dr. Burlingame came up the steps.

"Father!" she cried. "If I had only known you were looking for me! I wrote and you never answered and I thought you and Mother were angry at me for marrying Ray."

For a moment he could not answer. It must have been hard for him to realize that all his trouble had been caused by a simple mistake, a letter that had miscarried, a girl who hadn't understood how much her parents loved her. When she had kissed her father she turned to Judy, her eyes filled with tears of remorse.

"What a mistake girls make when they run away and get married," she said. "Ray and I could have waited. It's too late to make it up to Mother but we're going to see to it that Father never has a single worry from this day on. A girl owes it to her parents to stay with them until she's at least twenty."

"I think so too," Judy agreed with a fond look toward her own father.

"Judy, come here," cried Sally from the hammock where she was now sitting happily beside the lost uncle she had found. He was touching her hair with his fingers, seeing her as the blind do, with his sense of touch. But Judy, as she welcomed him, was thinking of still another surprise—Dr. Burlingame's experiment. Now they all knew that it had not been too late. Soon Lou Vincent would see again but, in the meantime, Sally promised to be his eyes. She took his arm as they all went inside a little later to have the tea that Mrs. Bolton had thoughtfully prepared. Peter, Horace and Honey came in together and Judy told Peter that he was really the cause of Dr. Burlingame's vanishing before he had time to open the door to his own kitchen.

"Gosh! I'm sorry," Peter began.

"That's all right, my boy," Dr. Burlingame stopped him. "You're more than forgiven. There are others around here, I'll warrant, with stranger things than that to tell."

He was right. Ray Suffern had been waiting for an opportunity to tell his story.

When they had all grouped around the fireplace, he was ready to begin. As the day was cool, Dr. Bolton lighted one of the smaller logs from the fallen tree while Horace threw the cretonne cover over the cage to make sure there would be no interruptions from his ill-mannered parrot. Blackberry came and sat by the fire just as if he knew that he, too, had played a large part in the unfolding drama. Although everybody was listening, Ray Suffern spoke directly to Judy.

"You guessed right, Miss Bolton," he said. "The car got out of control and Lou and I had to jump for our lives. I watched it roll into the river and then I turned to him and said, 'We'd be in there except for the grace of God.' Well, Lou stood thoughtful-like for a minute and then he said I shouldn't have saved him. He'd be better off dead than blind, he said. We got to talking like that and all at once I thought of a way out. I had an offer of a job in South America but my folks had different ideas. They had me all set to marry into a rich family. I knew they'd be deciding things for me all my life but here was one thing I could decide for myself and then, just as though the fates had sent her to me, along came Alice Burlingame, the girl I really cared for. She was driving a nifty little car of her own and picked us up. We told her the big idea and she was a romantic kid and it appealed to her.

" 'I'll send Father a note and we'll run away,' she said. Well, she did send it to him. She sent it by a little kid and gave the kid a dollar to deliver it.''

"The kid," said Lou Vincent grimly, "was my nephew Dickie. He's my brother Harry all over again. Couldn't be honest if he wanted to. Well, he must have turned the note over to his father——''

"And all this time they knew you were alive and never told anybody because they wanted your property. That's too awful!" gasped Judy. "And you're his own brother!"

"Cain was Able's brother too," Lou reminded her, "but that didn't stop him from rising up against him and slaying him. There's been dishonesty in the world ever since time began and it looks as though there always will be. But I had done about enough of assisting my brother in his crooked schemes. You can't realize, you people who can see, how wonderful it is to be blind and yet to suddenly see the way ahead so clearly. I never knew where I was going before. I had just followed Harry's directions. But that accident with the furniture polish brought me to my senses. I wanted nothing more to do with a factory that underpaid and endangered the lives of its employees. I was involved too deeply to get out any other way and Ray had told me there was work a blind man could do in the South American mines. The little hoard of money I had kept in the emergency box paid our passage. You found the note I had left for Sally. It wasn't until after her father died that I realized she was in trouble. Occasionally we managed to get hold of a Farringdon paper and Alice would read it to me. She missed the notice of her mother's death and I only learned of Ned's death through this will of mine that Harry decided to bring up in court. Then I knew I must come back and help Sally. It never occurred to me that I'd scare anybody until Sally was so terrified. Nobody seemed to want us and we were about to take the boat back to South America when I heard a newsboy shouting my name. I stopped him and asked him what it was all about and he read me the headlines.''

Judy shot her brother a triumphant glance. The story they had written up together had done exactly what they had meant it to do—and more. It had also brought back Dr. Burlingame's daughter. Judy could tell by the gleam in Horace's eyes that he was already anticipating a still bigger story. The following day it was

spread all over the front page of the paper.
Mr. Lee, the editor, was jubilant.

"Any time you're tired of law," he told Judy,
"there's a desk waiting for you in the Herald
Office."

"I appreciate your offer, Mr. Lee," she
smiled at him, "but not before Peter's next case
comes up—not for a desk at the White House.
This time when we fight Harry Vincent in the
court room we're going to win."

That evening when she told Peter about it
his face grew serious.

"Judy, if this job with me is ever keeping you
from anything bigger that you want to do——"

"Goose!" she scolded him. "There's only
one bigger job I can think of and, according to
Alice, I'm too young for that. Anyway, just for
the present, I'd rather be your secretary."

But they were both thinking of the future as
they walked out on the porch together and stood
gazing out across the valley that held the city of
Farringdon. It was just twilight and the view
was nicest then. Beyond the turrets of the
palatial Farringdon-Pett dwelling they could
see the courthouse clock with its illuminated
face. Soon Peter would be standing before the

rail in that solemn court room. Judy's heart swelled with pride at the thought.

"Justice, when equal scales she holds, is blind," she quoted softly. "You know, Peter, it was almost like blind Justice walking into this case when Lou Vincent returned. But his brother Harry is really the blind one. I feel so sorry for people who think money and property are more important than the ones they love——"

Her voice trailed off as Peter's arm encircled her.

"We'll never think that, will we, Judy? We'll keep on winning all our cases, even the ones we lose, so long as we never let ourselves think that."

Peter, however, did not lose his case when it came up for trial. No judge in the country would have decided in Harry Vincent's favor after hearing all the evidence Judy and Peter had against him. Long before the trial was finished everybody knew that Lou Vincent would recover all the property that had once been his. With his sight restored he was able to inspect the houses on upper Grove street and recommend many needed improvements. On these tours of inspection he was usually accompanied by Sally.

"I'm not used to seeing things for myself," he explained one evening when he and his niece stopped in, as they often did, to talk things over with Judy.

"That's just his way of telling you he's come for advice again," laughed Sally, "but this time I've already decided for him. He's moving out all that lovely furniture that's been stored in Dr. Burlingame's house for so long. You see, we're furnishing my house—the one my father left me. Uncle Harry had to move out, you know."

She did not add that her uncle Harry had moved so far away that it was quite probable she would never see him again, but Judy knew it was true. The name Vincent would now stand for Lou Vincent, the new president of the Farringdon Furniture Factory.

"Well, Judy, what I'm trying to tell you is that Uncle Lou thinks he'll be in the way. But I've decided the whole thing," she declared with spirit. "Dr. Burlingame and Ray and Alice and Uncle Lou and myself make a simply grand family. That house is too big for just a few people and we all get on so nicely. Dr. Burlingame's own house is much too lonely and, anyway, it's in bad shape and too far away from the main road to be of much use to a doctor. And, while we're moving things, we wondered if you wouldn't like something—just anything, you know, from among all those treasures.''

She found it hard to go on. Her heart was too filled with gratitude for words to come easily. But Judy understood.

"You want to reward me," she said, "just as if seeing you so happy isn't reward enough. Besides, your uncle gave Peter the chance he wanted and now he is improving upper Grove street and making one of my fondest dreams come true. Sally, you don't know how happy that makes me.''

"But I want to make you happier still," she insisted. "Without your help we might never have found each other. Judy, you did like the lamp, didn't you? And the candlesticks?''

"What about Lord Byron?" asked Lou Vincent. "That's as fine a piece of marble as you'll ever find and some day when you and that clever lawyer friend of yours are married and have a home to yourselves——''

"Now wait a minute!" Judy stopped him. "You're not to go into the matchmaking business, Mr. Vincent. I thought you were dealing strictly in furniture.''

"And statues—if you like them."

"I love Lord Byron," she exclaimed. "You couldn't have offered me anything that would have pleased me more. You see, Peter and I played he was our host that day we found Sally. It was exciting, wasn't it? And romantic," she added, smiling at the man whose deep-set blue eyes now saw everything so clearly, "but I never dreamed it would turn out so wonderfully for all of us."

And little does Judy dream, now, of the very exciting adventure that lays ahead of her told about in the next book, "The Name on the Bracelet."

THE END